CHAPTER ONE

They smelled the town before they saw it. It was a bad smell, damp, fishy and miserable, hanging like fog over the road. They heard the town before they saw it, the shrill calls of thousands of seagulls circling above. At the top of the hill the car paused. The car looked official, like it might belong to the government, unmarked and neutrally coloured. It had never travelled this road before, it was a stranger's car. Below, the road sharply descended into the town. There were two people in the back seat, a boy named Ewan and his mother, a frail, worried-looking woman.

'This is it,' said their driver, 'the end of the road.'

The driver was a plain-clothed policeman. He placed his arm over the front passenger seat and looked at the two in the back. His suit was the same colour as the car. 'I'm going to be honest with you,' he said, 'this town has a bad reputation, but nobody will find you here, that's for sure.'

Ewan's mother looked at her son for some sign of approval. He stared out of the window.

'Ever seen the Atlantic before?' the driver asked the boy.

'No,' then silence.

'Doesn't say much your lad, does he?' said the driver.

'No, not lately.'

'I don't want to be here,' said Ewan, to show he could talk if he wanted to.

Ewan pretended not to look, but he surveyed

1

the view through the window. The town was in a bay. Ewan could see its rocky mouth, half as far away as the horizon. Beyond was the grey Atlantic, brooding and big. To the right and left, on the hilltops, were a handful of small farms. Below was the town. The driver released the handbrake and they descended into it.

This was Ballydog.

The town square was at the water's edge, it was mainly just used for car parking. From there a few streets curved up the hillsides. There was a church, a school, a small housing estate. In the middle of the town was a huge square building, it stood like a god above everything else. A chimney in its roof pumped black fumes. This was the fish finger factory. It was a bad factory and the main source of the stink pervading the town. Any seagull that accidentally flew into the fume cloud would fall out of the sky dead. The factory had a janitor and one of his duties was to sweep up the dead seagulls piled at the foot of the chimney by the end of each day.

Some said the seagulls went into the fish fingers.

A pier jutted from the square two hundred metres out over the water. It stood on concrete piles set into the floor of the bay. The Ballydog fishing fleet was tied up there, more than a dozen trawlers of iron and fibreglass painted blue, green, black, red and yellow. These boats were the brightest splash of colour in Ballydog, Ewan could not hide his interest in them as they drove through the square, but it was a bad fleet. There was not a skipper on any of those boats who would not slash the nets of the others if he thought he would get away with it.

2

THE BADNESS OF BALLYDOG

Garrett Carr

First published in Great Britain in 2010
by Simon and Schuster UK Ltd
A CBS COMPANY
This Large Print edition published 2013
by AudioGO Ltd
by arrangement with Simon and Schuster UK Ltd

ISBN: 978 1471 303388

Text copyright © 2010 by Garrett Carr

www.garrettcarr.net

British Library Cataloguing in Publication Data available

Printed and bound in Great Britain by
MPG Books Group Limited

On one side of the square was the Ballydog Hotel, it was a bad hotel and always empty. Next door was the Lobster's Cage pub, a bad pub, but always full. Past the pub a street quickly narrowed and headed towards the lighthouse. The stranger's car did not travel this way, no car could. The road turned into a narrow track that ran between the rocky shore and rushy slopes. The lighthouse was out of sight of Ballydog, except at night when the pulse of its light could be seen in the air. It was painted purest white and seemed all the whiter because it was one of the few buildings in Ballydog that was painted at all. Mr Weir, the lighthouse keeper, proudly did the job himself, twice a year.

Between the lighthouse and the town square was the old pier, not used any more by fishermen since they got the new pier in the town centre. The old pier was made of rough blocks of stone. Rusted ladders and rings were bolted to its sides. Weeds grew from the gaps and at water-level generations of barnacles were clamped on top of one another. There was only one boat tied up at the old pier, a small fishing trawler called the *Sunny Buoy*. It had not moved in years.

A young girl, barefoot despite the cold, stepped out of the wheelhouse. She walked over to the railing and peered down into the water. Her name was May and the *Sunny Buoy* was her home.

'Good morning!' she said brightly, although no one else could be seen. 'A bit of breakfast?'

Under the grill in the wheelhouse over two dozen fish fingers were cooking. There was never a shortage of fish fingers in Ballydog. May went back inside to fetch a few, cupping them carefully in her hand so as not to get burned.

TERRRRR!

A seagull dive-bombed out of the sky and tried to steal the food.

'GET AWAY!' May yelled, leaning over to protect the feast. The seagull bounced off her back and spun away, shedding feathers. It circled her twice. She hissed at it. It gave up and went to join the flock wheeling above the town centre.

'That's right, scram,' said May, 'all ye think about is food.'

The squawking and screeching of seagulls was the constant soundtrack of Ballydog. They lived mainly off the fish spilling from trucks or left lying on decks at the end of each day. They squabbled over these pickings, two seagulls could often be seen pulling at the opposite ends of the same dead fish. If Ballydog seagulls heard that normal seagulls, from other parts of the coast, actually went out to sea and hunted fish for themselves they would not have believed it. They would have thought it was the craziest idea they had ever heard in their lives.

'Here ye go, Old Man,' May said and dropped a fish finger into the water. Two small fish darted towards the offering and nibbled at it.

'That's not for ye fellas, either,' she said.

The *Sunny Buoy* shifted in the water. Disturbed, the fish darted away. The car tyres hanging from the boat's side, to protect its woodwork from the rough stone, were pressed against the pier and squealed harshly. The old boards of the *Sunny Buoy* creaked. Underneath the hull something was waking up and beginning to move.

Foods, he was thinking.

One by one, May dropped more fish fingers into

4

the water.

* * *

On the other side of town the stranger's car cruised up Main Street and turned into the estate. The estate was spread over a hillside. There were about fifty grey houses in it.

'We've found you a place in here . . . somewhere,' said the driver.

It was a bad estate.

Every house was indistinguishable from every other. Every garden untended, every wall unpainted. Ewan saw people twitching their curtains to watch them go by. All day these people sought gossip, but very little ever happened to reward their spying. The stranger's car was the most interesting thing that had happened in weeks. The spies mostly spied on each other, then reported the information to someone who knew it already.

Ewan observed a group of boys about his age skulking along a street. They were kicking cans as they walked and they all had exactly the same haircut. This was Andrew and his pack. They were making their way home from school.

'Wait here,' Andrew said outside Kilfeather's grocery shop, 'I gotta get a cabbage for my ma.'

'Aren't you a good little boy getting the shopping?' said Mushroom, laughing. Andrew shot him a look that was enough to make him shut it.

'Only one of you boys at a time,' warned Mr Kilfeather, standing by the door in his brown shopkeeper's coat. 'Don't think I don't know who steals cigarettes on me.'

Andrew went in while the rest of the pack loitered outside, annoying Kilfeather by kicking at the coal bags stacked by the door.

'In my day you'd have been put to work in the fields,' said Kilfeather. He always said that.

'Come on, Kilfooler,' said Mushroom, 'we're products of society.'

Andrew dug through the cabbage display looking for one that was even half decent. Kilfeather was known to try and sell anything he could get away with. The joke in school was that he dyed Rice Krispies with mucky water and sold them as Coco Pops.

He heaved out one cabbage and shook the soil from it. A tiny centipede emerged from the leaves and ran across his finger. Andrew was no wimp but the sight of it caused him to jump with fright. He flung his hand away from him and the creepy-crawly hit the ground. Andrew glanced around to make sure nobody had seen him react like that.

He was relieved to see that nobody had.

The centipede started to straighten itself out. Andrew looked down at it. Then he stepped on it, grinding down with the sole of his shoe until the centipede was nothing but a stain on the floor.

*   *   *

The stranger's car moved to the far end of the estate, to the very last house, and stopped. The driver stepped out. He walked over to the 'For Rent' sign that stood in the front yard and pulled it out carefully, so as not to get dirt on his shoes.

'Here it is,' he said, smiling. He was trying to put a brave face on it.

6

Ewan and his mother pulled themselves from the back seat of the car. They were not happy about the house. They looked at it as if it was a gift they did not want. The driver pointed up to a large house overlooking the estate, its tall windows glinting. 'Your landlord's place,' he informed them. He glanced around to make sure nobody else was listening before saying, 'but you won't have to deal with him, we've already paid everything up.'

He went inside and Ewan's mother trailed in behind him.

Ewan stayed outside and looked back over the town. One word sprang to mind as he surveyed it. That word was *bad*.

Ewan's instincts were sharp. Ballydog was the baddest town in the country, possibly the world. There were no other towns within forty kilometres of Ballydog because nobody wanted to live within forty kilometres of it. It huddled in its harbour meanly, like a miser guarding his hoard. Even the weather seemed to dislike this town. Rain lashed down on it while the sun was shining everywhere else up and down the coast. Wind tried to blow its roofs off. Clouds hung low and sealed in the dampness. The town, as if attempting to have revenge on nature, used its fish finger factory to poison the sky. The farms grew nothing but discontent.

The people of Ballydog embodied the Seven Deadly Sins, and a few extra sins they had invented themselves. There was Manipulation, Grabbiness, Excessive Bossiness, Slimy Slipperiness, Aggressive Schemingness and Plain Dishonesty happening on every street everyday. But above all,

7

there was Badness. Anybody who wanted to be different in Ballydog needed to be careful. The town would work on them until they were broken and persuaded to see the world its way. Or it would just eat them for breakfast.

May was thirteen and small for her age. Her hair was mousy and unconsidered. She almost always wore a flower-print dress and a pair of wellington boots. Mostly she daydreamed. She had a secret friend who made her life bearable, but she kept secrets far greater than that.

Andrew was thirteen and the second tallest in his class. He was good at many things but not the kind of things you got homework in. He was good with spanners and drills. He understood pistons, rack and pinion and fuel injection. He was good at laying schemes and drawing diagrams. He rarely got into fights but had power. Most boys in Ballydog either feared him or were in his pack. Or both.

Ewan was also thirteen. His head was shaved. When standing still, he held his hands together in front of him, in the manner of a Buddhist monk. He moved quietly. Intelligent eyes watched everything from his inscrutable face. He had grown up in a city and knew nothing about fishing, milking cows, or other small-town things. His father was still back there, in detention and awaiting trial. Ewan and his mother had been sent across the border and hidden by the police in a witness protection programme. Ewan did not want to be in Ballydog. He had wanted to be left at home so he could visit his father every day. That was a whole other story, to be told another time. Ewan was important in Ballydog for different

8

reasons.

Ewan, Andrew and May. All three were going to be important.

CHAPTER TWO

Somewhere in the South Atlantic an American nuclear submarine was hovering above the ocean floor. Its name was the USS *Deep Trouble*. It was sitting still while awaiting new orders. Night had descended but it was always night this deep; sunlight could not reach there. From outside, the submarine looked like a giant, sleeping, metal monster, one-hundred-and-ten metres in length. Along the steel gangways of the *Deep Trouble* snores could be heard, while in the rec room other crew members were playing poker.

On the bridge, which was in the tower midway along the length of the submarine, the radar officer had just read an unidentified object coming into range. His console began to emit beeps, five seconds apart. He positioned his hand above the alert button and peered closer at the screen, the green glow from it making him look like an alien. The approaching object was moving onto the screen rapidly. It was too wide to be a submarine and, if it kept coming, it soon would be too long as well. It was travelling along the ocean floor, directly towards them, and seemed to be in a hurry. The radar officer let his hand fall and everywhere, up and down the *Deep Trouble*, a loud whooping alert threw the crew out of their bunks and onto their feet.

Captain Reef sprang up in his bunk and pulled his cap down tight. He prided himself on being ready for unexpected action within seven seconds, even if he had been sleeping deeply. He always slept with his uniform on. In the bridge the emergency lights had kicked in. Everything was bathed in red or lost in shadow. Officers crowded around the radar console. The thing was still coming and it outsized them substantially. This was a new situation; the *Deep Trouble* had never encountered anything bigger than itself before. If the thing struck them they would probably be doomed.

'Engines. Full. Reverse,' ordered Captain Reef. Down in the body of the submarine the engines rose to full power. Energy pulsed through the whole length of the craft, smooth but hugely powerful. But a machine the size of the *Deep Trouble* does not go from dead stop to full reverse in mere seconds. Painfully slowly the submarine began its retreat. Its nose dipped slightly as it crept backwards.

'Crew. Ideas,' demanded the Captain. He pulled his cap down tighter.

The crew did not have any ideas. They had never seen anything like this in their lives. It was too big to torpedo, it was the width of an airstrip. The beeps from the radar console were now coming three seconds apart.

'That's great, boys,' scoffed Captain Reef. 'Medals for the lot of you.'

The thing on the screen was now five kilometres long. It still kept coming.

'Lights. External. Full,' ordered the Captain. He pulled his cap down tighter. There was a dry *clunk*

10

sound and the *Deep Trouble* lit up like a Christmas tree. One powerful beam cut through the black and exposed a circle of sandy ocean floor beneath.

It may have been the lights that made the thing do what it did next, something that made the officers gasp, apart from Captain Reef who never gasped. The thing turned in a new direction, but not in the stiff way a submarine would: it *curved* itself into a new course as if it was a train, or a six-kilometre centipede. There was now a chance the thing might pass in front of their bow instead of hitting them. It would be very close, though. Maybe too close.

'One minute and closing, Captain,' reported the radar officer. The beeps now arrived two seconds apart. Sand on the ocean floor, lit with the submarine's spotlight, was shaking and rising. A gang of sharks burst into the cone of light. Great Whites, which do not usually swim in packs. They slowed a split second, dazzled by the unexpected brightness, then escaped to the other side of the light. The crew of the submarine could not escape so quickly, they could only hope to survive the colossal object racing in their direction.

The submarine was slammed from the side by a monstrous force. Not the thing itself but a wall of water pushed ahead by its charge. The submarine was thrown starboard and the crew bounced off the sides like rubber balls.

'Twenty-five seconds, sir,' yelled the radar officer as he struggled back to his feet. The beeps were less than a second apart. Another wall of water threw them further to starboard. Then another hit. It was as if the whole ocean had decided it wanted to be somewhere else. The crew

11

hung onto anything they could. The *Deep Trouble* was being turned and they were unable to do anything about it. Four more slams and the submarine had done a complete revolution.

'*It's right in front of us!*' screamed the radar officer, but where was front? Nobody could tell any more. The beeps merged into one continuous squeal burning in their ears. The submarine was spinning. The crew at the far ends were pinned to the walls and vomiting on their uniforms. Around and around it went. Nobody knew how many times. It was a nightmare ride on a forty-five-million-dollar merry-go-round that they could not get off.

Close by, the thing passed, cutting a deep swathe in the seabed and sending the ocean around it into a swirl. It was the biggest living thing on the face of the earth and if it knew about the trouble it was causing, it would not have cared.

Many of the crew had passed out by the time the *Deep Trouble* stopped revolving. They slid down the walls and lay in heaps. Others pulled themselves to their feet and rubbed their heads. It took a while for the dizziness to subside. Down beneath them, a great trench had been carved into the ocean floor, heading north. Every conscious person from bow to stern, every officer on the bridge and even Captain Reef himself was asking the same question: what *was* that thing?

CHAPTER THREE

Andrew awoke with a start so powerful it threw him out of bed. He sat up on the carpet. It had been a nightmare. *No . . . not a nightmare*, he told himself, *just a dream*. A bad dream.

He was standing at the end of a pier . . .

He forced himself to stop remembering the dream. It was better to ignore it.

Downstairs, the house was quiet; both his parents were already at work and his little brothers in playschool. The silence made him uneasy. He switched on the television. The screen filled with two heads nattering at each other in a pink and yellow studio. He looked at them for a while but did not really hear what they said. He ate some cornflakes, looked for his shirt and at nine minutes to nine he left the house.

He burst into his classroom eight minutes later. Just on time, as usual. A boy he had never seen before was standing in front of Heiferon's desk, getting a grilling. The new boy did not seem rattled by Heiferon. *Maybe he can join the pack*, thought Andrew. Then again, it was not good to have a pack member that was too tough or too smart, and certainly not both. Andrew sat at his desk and began waiting for break.

'So you're the new boy from the North,' Heiferon said, 'I was warned about you. Listen up now, bucko. I run a tight, businesslike operation here and I intend keeping it that way.'

Ewan noted the cracks in the windowpanes, the scribbles on the walls and the racket the rest of the

13

class were making behind him, but he decided not to mention them. He decided to say as little as possible. This was his first morning in Ballydog Secondary.

'You've probably grown up on government handouts. That's how it is in the North. I've been there. Once. Terrible place. Nothing but unemployed people, sitting around twiddling their thumbs and developing *the quare ways*. It's different here. Grow some hair, bucko, that's my first executive order. You want to fit in, don't you? And smarten up. Do you know how we survive in the wilds of the west? With our wits, you hear, bucko? OUR WITS!'

Heiferon threw himself a few centimetres out of his chair to try and scare the new boy. Ewan stood firm. The teacher was like a bulldog behind a fence. He even looked like one. The folds of flesh on his face drooped as if they wanted to be on the floor. *Does he use a towel when he gets out of the shower*, Ewan wondered, *or just shake himself dry?* Heiferon's suit could have been better dried. Ewan could smell the damp tweed from where he stood. Heiferon's glasses hung around his neck. They would not go on his face all day. At night, however, he wore them while constructing mousetraps of ingenious cruelty. Designing the perfect mousetrap was how Heiferon planned to get rich. He made prototypes with pins, matches, razor blades and rubber bands, they were said to be frightening to look upon.

'Do you know what the most important school subject is, bucko?' Heiferon said. 'It's business studies. Business drives everything in life, so I like to put business in every class I teach. This

14

conversation we are having right now is business. You are trying to *consolidate your resources* but this is my *hostile takeover*. You are going to learn a lot from Ballydog.'

Pleased, Heiferon sat back in his chair. Ewan groaned inwardly. Everything was worse than he had predicted. He was already having a bad day. He did not yet know that every day was a bad day in Ballydog.

'Tell me; what do you think the enemy of business is?' Heiferon was asking. 'Go on, do you have a tongue in your head at all?'

Ewan thought for a few moments. 'Dishonesty?' he suggested.

Heiferon sighed. 'No, no,' he said. 'Dishonesty is the lubrication of business. You need to smarten up, bucko. Do you know who your role model should be? A ROLE MODEL TO ALL OF YOU!' he shouted to be heard by the rest of the class. They carried on messing about regardless.

'Mr Fitzpatrick, business genius,' he went on. 'Born and raised in this very town, still lives here. I would invite him to come up and speak to the whole class, only I'm sure he is too busy to speak to such a PACK OF WASTERS!'

Heiferon focused on Ewan again. His eyes tightened as if he was looking at a tiny object. 'I can see it in you, bucko,' he said, *'the quare ways.'*

A silence hung between them for a few moments then Heiferon barked, 'You! Shove over and let the Northboy in beside you.' He was pointing at a boy in the front desk. 'But be careful, he has *the quare ways* about him. It can catch like the flu.'

Andrew moved over to let the new boy share his

desk, but he had already decided he wanted nothing to do with him. He did not even glance at Ewan as he sat down.

At break time the intercom units around the school made a loud burping sound. The students leaped up, tore out of the classrooms, rolled down the hall and tumbled into the yard. The yard was grassy until the maintenance man got tired of cutting it and one day covered it in concrete. There was one tree in the yard. Students stood under it when it rained, but it did not offer much shelter. It had not sprouted a leaf in seven years.

Once in the yard Ewan immediately had his back forced against the wall. The boys of his class moved in around him and fired questions at him, questions not asked out of interest but aimed to uncover weakness. They came thick and fast and were barely intended to be answered at all. One boy was nicknamed Mushroom, he was pale, thin and evil-eyed. He was the cleverest thirteen-year-old in Ballydog. Or at least he had been until Ewan moved to town.

'Don't mind Heiferon,' said Mushroom, 'he'll get bored of torturing you in a week or two.'

Ewan wondered if perhaps this was friendliness.

'Ourselves on the other hand,' Mushroom went on, 'we'll probably keep torturing you until the day you die.'

Perhaps not.

'Northboy lives in Prendergast's old house,' another boy said. 'I saw them moving in from my window. Didn't have much stuff, just one suitcase between them.'

'Instead of watching, you should have come over and said hello,' said Ewan.

16

This comment baffled the boys.

'Why would anybody do that?' asked Mushroom.

'To be neighbourly,' said Ewan.

The pack fell about laughing. 'Neighbourly! What a weirdo!'

Ewan was sick of all this by now. He put on a tough guy routine that he had practised. He stared at the pack until they stopped laughing. Slowly and deliberately, he stepped away from the wall and the boys, without even noticing, all took a step backwards.

'This has got boring,' said Mushroom. 'Catch you later.'

The boys wandered over to the boiler house, a small building that housed the heating generator for the school. Andrew was leaning against the wall with his hands in his pockets.

Ewan was left alone. He stayed where he was and looked around. It was the quietest schoolyard Ewan had ever witnessed, everyone was whispering. There were a lot of gangs and each seemed to be plotting something against the others. There were also a few outcasts, loners drifting around the walls and in between the pack territories. He recognised one as being a girl from his class. Her desk was at the back of the classroom, next to a window. Nobody sat beside her. Now she was looking intently up at a crow perched on the wall. She wore a dress and wellington boots, and gave such an impression of oddness she may as well have been wearing a giant yellow hat.

The schoolyard loners and the packs reminded Ewan of nature documentaries filmed in Africa, the way big cats, cheetahs and the like, would go for the weaker caribou that fell behind and were exposed. In the African savannah the loners would get picked off, whereas in Ballydog they just got picked *on*. Andrew led a gang. Nature documentaries would have called him, 'the alpha male'. Ewan watched Andrew and five of the boys disappear around the back of the boiler house.

'You're the new fella in town,' a girl's voice said from behind Ewan. 'Ye live in a house with no furniture in it because ye had to move in a hurry. When ye left your house this morning your mam stood at the door and watched ye leaving. Then she stayed standing there in the door for a long time and—'

The girl stopped mid-sentence when Ewan turned around. She looked anxious, as if she had said too much. It was the loner girl.

'I suppose you live on my street too?' said Ewan, annoyed.

She backed away so quickly she almost tripped over her wellingtons. 'No,' she said, 'a wee bird told me.'

The intercom burped and the break was over.

CHAPTER FOUR

May was the keeper of secrets, secrets she could barely understand herself.

Of all the youngsters of Ballydog Secondary, May had the longest walk home. It did not bother her. She liked it. Especially the last kilometre when there was nothing but rocky shore on one

18

side and rushy slopes on the other. The rushes were a hardy type of grass that grew near the sea despite stiff breezes and land full of sea salt. It grew in tufts and was itself tough. Walking by, May felt the company of snails in the rushes and the presence of scuttling crabs on the shore. On a very peaceful day she could even experience a mind-tingle from the barnacles clinging to the stones.

Everybody in Ballydog knew that May thought she could understand animals. This made her soft in the head as far as they were concerned, fit only for laughing at. They never asked for the details. For one thing, May never claimed to *understand* animals. She was not some kind of Dr Dolittle. It was more that animals were a kind of window on the world for May. She came to understand things through them.

For example, that morning a crow had stood on Ewan's roof. Later that same bird landed on the school wall and May saw it. Yet she saw more than just the crow. She tuned into it, the way you might tune into a radio station. Through the crow, in a method beyond science, May came to know things about the new boy.

Or was she just mad?

Sometimes May feared the town's people were right. She was 'soft in the head'. It was not just the Ballydog folk that thought so. The Woman from Health would drive in over the hill once a week especially to see her. The Woman from Health told her that the ideas she got from animals were all actually invented in her head, and she was a doctor with many letters after her name. She gave her little pills to take. Often May believed her and took her pills. On the days May believed that everyone was right about her she would become very afraid of what her mind was doing to her. She would spend days without speaking, mistrusting everything, especially herself.

May approached the old pier and the *Sunny Buoy* tied up there. All day and night the trawler rose and fell with the tides. The car tyres protecting the sides were being slowly ground away and in few more years would be completely gone. Its mast was warped, its engine rusted and seized up. On damp days, which was most days in Ballydog, the eggy smell of wood rot hugged the boat.

Eleven years before, May's mam had left. That day her dad tied up the *Sunny Buoy* with knots never untied since. Shortly afterwards they began to actually live on the boat. May's room was the wheelhouse. A hammock was her bed. The toilet and washroom jutted out the back of the wheelhouse, the size of a wardrobe. Her dad slept in the rear hold, a very cramped space. *Sunny Buoy* was hardly an ideal home but it still made May happy to step on the deck and feel the boat move with the sea.

She went to the back of the wheelhouse and uncovered the generator. She gave its cord four or five sharp tugs before it spluttered into life. It settled into a happy chugging rhythm and there was electric power again.

In the wheelhouse, May dropped her school bag by the wheel, not to be touched again until the next morning. She switched on the grill and lined up twenty-five fish fingers on the tinfoil. The smell of fish and hot oil drifted about. From under her feet she felt a large living presence. It was

20

dreaming.

'Ah . . . hello, May.'

Her dad was stepping onto the deck. He seemed embarrassed to see her, as if he was doing something wrong. It was true he should normally be working at this time.

This is bad, thought May. She did not want him to be there. She did not want her dad to know about *him* below. She tried to act natural.

'Hello, Dad.'

'I had to come home to put on my spare set of overalls,' he said 'I got some nasty chemical spilt on me and was told to change.' He laughed, although it was not particularly funny. There was a bright yellow splash, as thick as paint, across his overalls.

'It's getting dark early these days, eh?' he said. 'Let's get this light on.'

He pulled the heavy switch of the mast-light. The switch clunked home and fired a couple of sparks. The spotlight washed the deck with a tungsten orange glow. The light also reached a couple of metres down into the water.

Oh no, thought May, *that will wake him up*.

'So . . . how was school?' her dad asked.

'Fine,' shrugged May. 'Same as usual.'

'Good, good,' he said and went around the back of the wheelhouse, unbuttoning his overalls.

Under the hull the large shape shuddered. He was stirring.

'I'll be a wee bit late getting back tonight,' her dad said as he changed.

May did not know why he told her, it was almost always the case. He would go straight into the Lobster's Cage after work and drink until he was

21

thrown out. Sometimes whole days could go by without May and her dad seeing each other. She was long past being heartbroken about this. It was life.

Just go, she willed him. *Just go . . .*

For three months now she had had someone else keeping her company.

'That's a lot of fish fingers you have on the go,' said her dad, coming back around the wheelhouse.

'Aye, I'm fierce hungry,' said May.

Under the hull the life form stretched out his neck.

Her dad said no more about the fish fingers. To him his daughter was a collection of mysteries. With an awkward smile he left. May watched him go.

Inside, May put all the grilled fish fingers on a plate. Then she walked around the raised covering of the *Sunny Buoy*'s engine, in the middle of the deck, and dropped a fish finger in the water. It began to sink. Usually little fishes would approach to nibble at these gifts but this evening none appeared. A large dark shape moved from under the boat. It was as if a part of the underwater shadow cast by the hull had decided to break off and be its own shadow somewhere else. May had already seen the Old Man of the Sea, as she had named him, many times but her heart skipped to see him again. He took the fish finger in his beak and slowly pushed to the surface. May encouraged him up with more food. From above he was the size of a small car. His flippers were the size of cupboard doors and his shell was like the valleys and ridges of some strange dark planet. He was a leatherback turtle, a big one.

Foods, he was thinking, *without efforts*, and *good*.
'My pleasure,' said May.

She dropped fish fingers into his mouth. He gulped them down in great old-man gulps. His shell carried scars. The teeth marks of a killer whale, and the single deep score of a propeller blade. He had survived these encounters and, despite his scars, he was a graceful old creature. He rested at the water's surface, looking up at the girl.

'Did you miss me?' asked May.

Foods, he was still thinking.

This leatherback was far from his usual migration routes. His age may have meant he was not as good a navigator as he once was. Also, warm currents reached further north now than ever before and this may have confused him. He had swum into the bay a few months earlier, found the old pier and taken shelter there. May had felt his presence the moment she had come back from school. She had never felt anything like it before. The Old Man of the Sea helped her believe in herself and her special link with the animal kingdom. When she was with him she knew she was not soft in the head. May was sure her mind could not invent the visions the leatherback passed to her. His life flowed into her with a clarity she had never experienced before. It was actually like being spoken to. She spent all day looking forward to seeing him when she got home. May hoped he would stay for good.

May fed him more, then just leaned on the railing and watched him, listened to him, went places with him as his mind wandered.

The golden shores of southern islands.

The black depths of the ocean.

*　　　*　　　*

After dinner Andrew helped his mother clean up. He plonked his twin brothers down in the midst of the building blocks spread behind the sofa in the living room. They smiled up at him gratefully and he ruffled their hair. His father, still smelling faintly of fish from his day out at sea, switched on the news and settled in for the evening. There was always plenty of bad news on the telly and he could not get enough.

'Da, do you want anything done in the garage?' called Andrew, after the dishes were done.

'Nope,' the silhouette of his head replied from the sofa.

Andrew put on his coat and went out.

'Where do you think Andrew's going?' whispered one little brother to the other.

'To The Villa,' the other replied.

In the trees between the estate and a lane called the Batter, stood The Villa. Andrew and his pack were there most nights. It was built of wooden pallets, borrowed barrels and large sheets of dirty plastic used as roofing. This was where Andrew and his pack planned acts of badness. Eight or nine boys made up the core of the gang but the number could vary as daily power struggles were won and lost. Andrew reigned supreme in The Villa. It was he who decided things or, at least, he always created that impression. Andrew was not boss because he was strongest, nor because he had the best ideas, it was because he could feel the mood of the pack better than any of them. He knew what

24

they wanted to do before they did themselves. The pack loved him for that. They all waged little wars with each other to gain favour with him. They dealt, backstabbed and traded. Their currency used to be the marble, but had recently converted to the cigarette.

A few metres from The Villa, Andrew paused, leaned against a tree and listened to the chat and laughter of the pack. It sounded as if they were all already there. This was good. Andrew liked being the last to arrive. It suited his position as leader.

The Villa was lit with County Council warning lights, stolen from roadworks, and strings of Christmas lights. The electricity needed to run the lights was brought to The Villa by means of twenty extension leads, plugged together to form one extremely long cable. It ran a couple of centimetres under the soil down to the back of the estate. From there it ran up through a hole in the back window of Miss Grope's garage. Unknown to Miss Grope, the cable was plugged into one of her garage's electrical sockets. Andrew and the pack knew she would never discover this uninvited plug as she was old, half-blind and afraid to go near her garage anyway. She believed it to be haunted. It was Andrew's pack that put this idea in her head. On the night of tapping her power supply they daubed evil-looking symbols on Miss Grope's garage door, strange runes and backwards letters in black paint. She never went in there again.

Making Miss Grope think there was something sinister about her garage was unnecessary and excessive. Her age and short-sightedness meant she was unlikely to discover their cable anyway. Did the boys really have to almost give her a heart attack with those frightening symbols? No, they did not. Then why did they do it? For badness, that is why.

'All right, lads,' said Andrew as he entered.

'All right, Andrew,' everyone except Mushroom replied.

Andrew noticed this but let it pass. Mushroom was trying to teach Tonne MacPherson to play backgammon. He was not having much success. MacPherson was not the cleverest.

'What'll we get up to tonight?' a boy asked.

'Maybe we'll chuck you in the bay,' said Andrew as he sat in his throne, the ripped-out seat of a Ford Fiesta. The rest of the pack laughed.

Andrew had no idea what tonight's amusements would be, but he was not concerned. He always thought of something in the end. They all just sat around a while. Andrew fed the goldfish. He ripped the pages from a copybook and perfected a paper-plane design. Then he passed more time by scribbling in the pages of the copybook, stolen off one of the younger kids in the schoolyard that day. He was only making meaningless doodles. Or at least he thought he was.

'That picture's brilliant,' said one of the boys to him ten minutes later. He was the newest boy to gain the right to enter The Villa. He was looking over Andrew's shoulder. Andrew hated that.

'Sure it's not even a picture,' said Andrew, 'only a scribble.'

'Naw, it's not,' insisted the new boy, 'look.' He picked up the book and held it in front of Andrew's face. 'See it? There's its mouth and there's its body. Is it a centipede, Andrew? Or a monster?'

26

Then Andrew saw it, looking back out of him from the midst of his scribbles. He had not even realised he had drawn it.

'It's really good whatever it is.'

Andrew jumped up, ripped the book from the boy's hand and flung it across The Villa. Everyone looked up. The boy retreated quickly, stammering and apologising. His attempt to gain favour with Andrew had gone badly wrong.

Andrew had gone quite stiff. His pack looked at him curiously. It was not like him to lose control. He forced a smile.

'All right, lads,' he said, 'let's get up to something then, will we?'

*   *   *

The Old Man of the Sea was drifting in and out from the side of the *Sunny Buoy*. It was now an hour since he had eaten and May knew he would soon get tired and seek shelter under the hull again. He only ever spent about an hour with May but it meant the world to her. He was like family. It was quality time. It occurred to May that when he was at his closest to the boat she might be able to pat him on the head.

'Come on in, fella,' she said, leaning over the railing.

He looked up at her.

What does the overlander want now?

When he had drifted near the hull May leaned over the railing and tested her balance. To reach the turtle's head she would have turn her body into a see-saw. Her feet would have to leave the deck and she would have to be careful not to go too far.

27

Beyond a certain limit she would lose her balance and fall into the water. Falling was not an option, as she could not swim. A strange situation for a girl living on a boat, but nobody had ever offered to teach her. Besides, Ballydog Bay was cold, oily and uninviting.

She held her breath, placed her weight on her stomach, stiffened herself from head to toe, and pivoted over the railing. She held one hand against the side of the boat to help her reach lower. Her acrobatics succeeded. She was able to firmly pat his football-sized head several times. It was smooth and wet like a living pebble. Then she pushed herself back up until her feet were on the deck again. Her heart beat hard. Touching a creature so rare was magical, like stroking the mane of a unicorn might be. The Old Man of the Sea liked the contact; she felt his pleasure.

He looked up at her again.

Cities of seaweed.

Fields of coral.

He twisted his head in the direction of the open sea.

There are things in my world no overlander can imagine.

CHAPTER FIVE

It took a month for the creature to wake up. Slowly it became aware of itself. Ancient instincts throbbed dully at the back of its tiny brain. It was deep down, the whole weight of the ocean on its back. It had not moved in so long that it was covered in layers of sand and coral. It had become a mountainous ridge in the seabed. After a few weeks it stretched itself. Six thousand tonnes of sediment was violently ruptured as a result of that yawn. Immeasurable amounts of sea life died in the quake; armies of crustaceans, tonnes of fish, an entire species of sea urchin. It was an ecological disaster no one ever heard of. The creature's eyes began seeing again. It had no eyelids; when it awoke, its brain and eyes just *switched on*.

It began to move. It travelled on the ocean floor, vast but completely hidden from the overworld. It went slowly at first. It would gather speed as its rage increased.

Over the centuries there have been many legends, stories and art works passed down featuring the sea creature. However, there has only ever been one written account from a person who actually saw it with his own eyes.

Low Too was an inventor who lived in China six hundred years ago, during the Ming dynasty. He played a part in the development of the air bellows, the compass and the diving bell. In a diving bell a person could descend to the sea floor and remain there for as long as they wished. Like a church bell, it was strong, moulded of thick iron but open at the base. Low Too's prototype was big enough for one person to sit in. It had a porthole with glass five centimetres thick on one side and a tube coming from the top to supply air to the sub-mariner. The whole craft was raised and lowered from a boat.

Low Too and his support crew travelled two kilometres off shore. The device, with Low Too in it, was lowered to the seabed. He stayed submerged for seven days and seven nights. It was a shallow patch of ocean, so he had enough light to observe the sea life. His undersea diary, still held by the Imperial Museum Beijing, contained many sketches of fish and poems written in their honour. He also made studies of swimming scallops and named a new species of octopus.

On the third day things got strange. The sea life thinned out and before nightfall there wasn't a single fish passing by his porthole. In the diary he recorded that a sense of unease built up inside him. He blamed it on the disappearance of the sea life. But what to blame the disappearance of the sea life on?

A couple of days later the seabed began to tremble. A huge living thing came into view. It was passing some kilometres away but Low Too could see it well through the crystalline water. It was extremely long, the whole length of the seafloor's horizon. It took half a day for it to pass. Thousands of marching legs propelled it. The ocean floor shook. Low Too feared that the bell would crack or flip over. Luckily, his diving bell withstood the pressure and he was able to witness the creature and survive the experience, he named it 古旅行者: The Ancient Traveller.

*   *   *

Carved into the stone of a Mayan temple in Guatemala, Central America, is a picture of the creature, looming out of the sea and about to swallow a sleeping village. Great gushes of water run from its body, sinking canoes. In the Mayan myth the creature was a destroyer of evil cities. They called it the Leveller.

Along Africa's Gold Coast, tales of the creature were told after sundown. The tribes knew the creature by a name that translates as, 'The ocean divides when it rises, it swallows you, your father, your mother, and your children and we will deny we ever knew you for fear of bringing bad luck upon ourselves'.

The small island of Tali, off the Colombian coast, was once one of a pair. Another island was a twenty-minute canoe ride across the shallows. It was called Blanco. Some old maps mark Blanco but the actual island is gone. Only the oldest people of Tali remembered Blanco, it was already starting to slip from belief. The old folks claimed it was visible on the horizon when they were children and it was an island of cruel and greedy people. It was eaten on a night of no moon, by a creature they called Big Hungry.

Whatever it is called, wherever it was from, the very same sea creature was now awake for the first time in eighty years. And it was aimed straight for Ballydog.

CHAPTER SIX

'You're the good draughtsman, aren't you, bucko?' Heiferon said to Andrew while placing a blank paper on the desk. 'I want you to draw a diagram of this for me.'

From a shoebox, Heiferon removed a delicate contraption of wire, springs and soldered joints and placed it in front of Andrew.

'The best mousetrap I've ever made,' he said.

'The perfection of a design I've been working on for years. Now ready to go public. I'm going to sell the design to mousetrap manufacturers and make a fortune. You'll be able to say you knew me when I was a teacher.'

Ewan looked at the mousetrap. He did not think it had a future. He saw that Heiferon's design might be effective at stopping mice but would not be a success with the general public. Certainly thousands of people wanted to get rid of mice from time to time. They bought traps to catch them or even kill them. But Heiferon's mistake was believing that people wanted to take revenge on the mice that entered their homes. Ewan did not think this was the case. Nobody would buy a mousetrap that stabbed, hammered and then strangled a mouse like this one did. Ewan was sure that most people would find Heiferon's design excessively cruel. At least the people outside Ballydog would.

'I want to send a diagram of the design to the patent office,' Heiferon went on, 'so draw it up there, Andrew. One view from the top and one from the side. Get busy.'

Andrew was not easily shoved around. 'What's in it for me?' he said, and Ewan felt a moment of admiration.

Heiferon emitted a low, slow growl. 'How about I promise not to put you in detention every day for the rest of your, probably short, time in secondary education?' he said.

'My fingers hurt today, sir. Can't draw a thing,' said Andrew. He leaned back in his chair.

Heiferon laughed out loud. This was to show that although he had lost the argument he did not mind, in fact he was big enough to enjoy it. This was untrue, of course.

'All right, bucko, I'll give you five euro.'

'Deal,' said Andrew and while he sharpened his pencils, Heiferon plopped down behind his desk and went to sleep.

Ewan, happy to mind his own business, began reading but then, at the rate of one a minute, balls of paper began bouncing off his head. The boys and girls behind him were throwing them. He knew that informing Heiferon was not an option. The teacher was more likely to punish Ewan for interrupting his nap than going after the paper-chuckers. Andrew was not paying any attention to the persecution aimed at the boy beside him. He focused on his drawing completely, hunched close over the paper and working carefully with a pencil and a ruler. He looked like an engineer or architect. The diagram was good, well worth five euros.

Ewan could ignore the balls of paper but when the lunch box hit the back of his head he spun around in his seat. The plastic box clattered off the desk behind him. Heiferon shifted in his seat but did not open his eyes. The boys and girls grinned at Ewan.

'Face the board, Northboy, we know what you look like,' said Mushroom.

Ewan's hands turned to fists, but then the sight of the girl at the last desk had a calming effect on him. He had forgotten about that fragile-looking girl. How had she known those things about him? What she had said to him was all true. She still looked odd. Her arms hung by her sides and she was staring out the window, absorbed by seagulls fighting in the schoolyard. She was completely detached from the goings-on in the classroom.

A good idea, thought Ewan.

When Ewan turned back, he glanced at Andrew and found him greatly changed. Now Andrew was sitting up straight. No longer drawing in a careful, controlled manner, he had dropped the ruler and was drawing fast and loose, his pencil dancing across the sheet of paper. He was drawing something new directly on top of the unfinished diagram of the mousetrap. Ewan noticed a blank look in Andrew's eyes. He was not even blinking. He looked like a crazed artist, a wild spirit who would probably die young.

In light and jagged lines Andrew was drawing a sea creature of some kind. It was like a gigantic millipede. Uncountable legs stuck from along its length. It reared out of the sea, its body bent like a question mark. Its two blank eyes were on stalks; they reminded Ewan of surveillance cameras. It didn't have a head; instead its body just ended in a round mouth. From its throat sprang fifty tongues.

Then the smell of damp tweed was upon them. 'Andrew! What on earth have you done?' demanded the voice of Heiferon from above. Andrew snapped out of his trance and looked down in horror at what he had created. His pencil fell out of his hand.

'That is certainly *not* what I ordered. A beastie of some sort, is it?' demanded Heiferon. He was shaking with rage. 'What do you think you're at? Here!'

Heiferon snatched the sheet of paper from the desk. He tore at it in a frenzy while the class stared. He was not concerned about losing the

34

diagram of the mousetrap. He was desperate to get rid of the sea creature. He grunted and swore as he ripped at the page. Small strips of paper fell around his feet. Soon there was not a piece left that was bigger than a toenail. Andrew's head hung in shame but Heiferon was pleased that he had removed the horrible sketch from existence and strode back to his desk.

'Buckos and buckerettes, it is my duty to warn you about the dangers of the overactive imagination,' he boomed. This time everybody listened. 'It might *seem* like fun and games to begin with but once you have let it in it'll make a nest in your brain and you're finished. You'll have gone soft in the head.'

At this point Heiferon nodded towards May and everyone understood what he meant. May was still staring at the seagulls, oblivious to everything else.

Heiferon shuddered as if a cold wind had passed through his body. 'I'd rather have my arms and legs chopped off than have an overactive imagination,' he said.

It was a short lesson but Heiferon felt pride rise up in him. He sat down behind his desk and looked over his classroom. He knew that he was a tad lazy sometimes, and a little bad-tempered, but his heart was in the right place, was it not? Life was a tough business and who would prepare these youths if not he? He smiled to himself. He closed his eyes. He fell asleep again.

Andrew was red-faced. He picked up his pencil and gripped it in both his fists. He could not understand what was happening to him.

Ewan leaned over to him and said, 'I thought it was an excellent drawing.'

35

Andrew turned on his neighbour.

'Shut it, you. It was a rubbish picture, just something I made up. Heiferon is right. Don't be talking to me any more, I want nothing to do with you.'

With the show over and Heiferon snoring, the balls of paper began to rain down on Ewan again.

CHAPTER SEVEN

That evening on the *Sunny Buoy*, May cooked supper for herself and the Old Man of the Sea, exactly as she had done for months. She switched on the mast-light and began dropping the food into the water. As the turtle woke up and rose to the surface May began to read new thoughts from him, thoughts she did not like.

Foods . . . energy for travel, understood May. *I leave now . . . Danger approaches from south.*

May watched as he gulped down the fish fingers. He ate faster than usual. May realised he was not just leaving, he was leaving immediately.

'Don't go,' said May, suddenly lonely, 'what's this danger you're goin' on about? You're safe and sound here under me boat.'

Dark warnings filled her mind.

Big-Boss coming . . . I get out of its way . . . You should too. Go inside, to the hills. Ha! You think I mustn't know what are hills because I live in the underworld? We have hills in here too, we have mountain ranges. But nothing big enough to stop Big-Boss . . . It is angry and coming this way. It will swallow this whole coastline. Get out of the way is all we can do.

May did not understand any of this, and she did not care. She was concerned with the immediate problem. Her friend was leaving, he was leaving right now. She did not want to be left alone. The Old Man was revolving himself with one of his flippers. He pointed his beak towards the mouth of the bay.

'No, wait a wee second,' said May. She lunged over the *Sunny Buoy*'s side and reached out. She stiffened herself and did her impression of a see-saw so as to be able to touch him. May just managed to brush the top of his head and shell with her fingertips before he was beyond reach. With a massive four-flippered shove he pushed away seaward. May hung over the railing and watched him go. He slipped under the water leaving hardly a ripple, swallowed by darkness and depth. Gone.

Goodbye, she thought. The leatherback thought it too.

The next four or five seconds of May's life took longer than four or five seconds normally take. As if in slow motion May realised that her see-saw balance was gone. She was sliding off the railing towards the water. Desperately her arms swung out and around but her hands found nothing to grip. She was going to fall in and there was nothing she could do about it. She had time to feel frightened, stupid and very helpless, drowning was a definite possibility. Then she went under and the bay accepted her hungrily.

May's wellingtons filled with water and dragged her down. She felt strangely calm but very lonely; drowning is the loneliest way to die. The light from the boat meant May could see the stony floor beneath her, an orange light on the black underwater world. She saw dozens of crabs scuttling over the stones, heading towards open sea just like the turtle had. They were in lines like refugees leaving a war zone.

Escapebig-bossescapeescapeescapeescapebig-boss-escape.

May let out a gasp and water entered her lungs. Panicking, she began to thrash her arms, a dysfunctional imitation of what swimming might be like. Her fingers contacted the hull of the boat. It was rough with barnacles. She tore at them, trying to find grip. She cut the palms of her hands but found nothing to hold. The hull curved away from her as she sank deeper. Instinctively she pushed away from under the boat and fought for the pier instead. If only she could make it to a ladder on the side of the pier . . . if only.

But her mind and body were already separating. As her body sank her mind floated upward and she ceased to panic. There was salt water in her lungs and stomach. Her body went loose and scenes from her life flashed through her mind. It had been a short life, full of secrets.

There was a swirl of bubbles and action around her. Through the haze of drowning she felt the presence of something beside her. A presence that was somehow friendly.

Overlanders must know their correct place.

May received a whack from a flipper the size of a cupboard door. She was propelled through the water. She barely had time to raise her arms to protect herself before she hit the pier. Automatically she dug her fingers into gaps in the stonework and pulled herself up once, then another time. A third time and she broke the surface. It was like being born again. She retched up bay water and reached blindly for the ladder. Her fingers found the rusted metal and she pulled herself over onto it, still spitting out water. Then she hung there and breathed, just breathed, her wellingtons still on her feet and in the water. Her whole body ached from the whack, the whack that had saved her life.

Having done this favour to the overlander who had fed him, the Old Man of the Sea turned seaward again. This time he would not return for anything. May watched him go. A dull sense of shock settled upon her and she hung on the ladder a long time, not moving, not thinking. Her life was hers once again.

CHAPTER EIGHT

'What have we done to deserve this?' 'Nothing at all, nothing at all.' This was what the Ballydog folk were saying to each other the following afternoon when the fleet failed to bring back a haul. The sea around Ballydog was mysteriously empty of fish. Hardly a single cod, or a mackerel, or a whiting was netted that day. Nobody could remember anything like it ever happening before. The people did not ask what drove the fish away, nor what could be done to encourage them back. Instead they demanded, 'What have we done to deserve this?' Then replied as quickly, 'Nothing . . . nothing at all.'

In a normal day the fleet would race each other back into Ballydog Bay and the skippers of each vessel would jibe at each other over their short-band radios, each claiming to have found the biggest shoals of fish and brought home the biggest catch. Today was very different. Each trawler only had a few fish flopping about in their holds. As they motored for port the crews paced their decks and gave sharp kicks to empty crates. They blamed their faulty nets, they blamed Global Warming, they blamed the Spanish and they blamed the other boats of Ballydog. The skippers spoke to each other over their radios. They were suspicious of one another but knew it made no sense. They saw how high each boat was riding on the waves, each hold as empty as every other. There were simply no fish today. The fleet returned to Ballydog looking like an army that just lost a war.

After docking, some crewmen went straight to the Lobster's Cage. The machines in the fish finger factory rumbled like hungry stomachs but there was nothing to give them so they were powered down. May watched fishermen go into the bar from behind a pile of nets at the edge of the town square. For once May had not gone straight home to the *Sunny Buoy* after school. All day her head had been full of the Old Man's warning. She could think of nothing else, she had to talk to someone about this 'Big-Boss'. When the fishermen had gone she walked across the square and stood outside the fish finger factory. Its mouth-like entrance stood over the square, big enough for two trucks to pass each other without knocking their rear-view mirrors. On a normal day tonnes of fish would now be getting dumped in the factory and

40

truckloads of frozen fish fingers would begin pumping out the other side. Today was different. Although toxic smoke still rose from the factory's tall brick chimney.

May wanted to talk to her dad before he went to the Lobster's Cage, as he was sure to after clocking-out. The Lobster's Cage was between the factory and the beginning of the path to the old pier. It seemed to block the way home; if the bar was not on the way to the *Sunny Buoy* would her dad still go there every night? Sadly, the answer was probably yes. Already loud voices and arguments could be heard from inside the bar. Some of the fishermen were finding any excuse to fight after their frustrating day. May would rather do anything than step inside that frightening place. In her imagination it was like a black hole, or quicksand. It stole souls. Going to the Cage every evening was a habit that a lot of townsfolk had and would probably never break. Her dad was not the only one. To May it made no sense. They worked all day to earn the money to hand over the counter of the Lobster's Cage every evening. Their days were spent working, their nights spent in the Cage. In that dark place the customers all drank the same thing: Ponny Dew, a bitter and addictive yellow concoction. It smelled like chemical waste but was cheap and three pints was never enough. Conn McKann, the owner of the Lobster's Cage, mixed it himself.

There was no sign of anybody inside the factory. Its sheer size intimidated her as she entered, it seemed to swallow her up. Inside was the biggest room she had ever been in. It was bigger than the town hall, bigger than the church. The smell of industrial cleaning products mingled with the smell of yesterday's fish. There were huge steel vats on wheels and several forklift trucks parked here and there. In the centre of the factory was what you might call its heart: a towering complex of walkways, chutes and drums of mysterious purpose reaching to the ceiling. This was the centre of operations. Conveyor belts ran left and right out of the machinery and back to where the snap freezers were located. May felt the huge apparatus was a metal monster, a brooding and somehow dangerous thing that would keep on being dangerous even if all its plugs were pulled out.

There was no sign of anybody. It seemed all the employees had been let go for the afternoon because of the fish shortage. But May's dad was a janitor and he might not have gotten off just because everybody else had. The cleaning would still need to be done.

'Dad, are ye here still?' May's voice travelled across the huge chamber, echoed and faded. Nobody replied. Then she heard somebody approach from behind the machinery, footsteps reverberated in the otherwise silent hall. They took an age to arrive; May thought about running away. A man stepped from around the heart of the factory. He was not her father but his face was in shadow so May could not see who he was. For a moment an irrational fear of him bubbled up inside her but as he came closer she saw he was Mr Fitzpatrick, the owner of the factory, and she relaxed, a little. Ballydog's richest man carried with him the silvery aura of power. He did not just own the fish finger factory, he owned about half the town, including many of the houses up on the estate.

'Are you lost?' he asked.

He did not seem unkind. May had only ever heard her father say good things about Fitzpatrick, or Fitz as he was usually known. If not exactly good then not too bad, which was good in Ballydog.

'No, I'm looking for me dad, he works here,' she said.

'Well there's nobody here now, I let the lot of them off early. You might find him over there.' Fitz indicated towards the bar across the square.

'Daddy, where're the staff?' Cynthia Fitzpatrick had arrived. The *clack* of her heels resounded across the concrete floor. She dropped her school bag and gestured around the empty factory. She seemed excessively horrified at the lack of any work going on. May and Cynthia were in the same class but that afternoon Cynthia did exactly what she did during school hours, ignored May completely.

'Annoying, isn't it?' Fitz said, but he did not seem too concerned. 'You know this is the first time since opening that this factory hasn't been producing.'

' "*Annoying*"?' said Cynthia. 'Daddy, it's a disaster.'

May did not want to be there. She was spare to the scene but did not just want to turn her back on Fitz and walk away, wouldn't that be rude? She found herself admiring Cynthia's gleaming hair and her heeled shoes. The shoes, as black and shiny as her hair, were new and made Cynthia look tall, cool and adult.

'What are we going to do?' said Cynthia, as if

43

she was her dad's business partner.

Fitz laughed. 'The same thing I have always done. Take a problem and make it into an advantage.'

Cynthia huffed. 'How are we going to do that?'

'Something will turn up,' he said. 'It always does.'

With that he gave May a wink and walked back into the factory. Cynthia trailed after him, demanding he be more specific.

May walked over to the Lobster's Cage. She put her fingers, still scratched and hurting from the night before, to the windowsill, stood on the tips of her toes and looked under the curtains. It was hard to see anything through the small gap and thick bubbly glass, just the impression of yellow light and men's backs hunched around drinks. She could not bring herself to go in. Her dad would not want to see her in the Lobster's Cage, and she did not want to see him in there either. His hands would be wrapped around his glass as if it was all he had. She stepped away from the window and felt despair wash over her. She was alone and adrift, with nothing but badness all around.

May knew her dad would probably not have listened anyway. He would never believe anything passed to her from an animal. All she had to do was mention her link with animal life and he would turn pale. He was ashamed of her, she knew it. So who could she turn to? Could the 'Big-Boss' be a real thing? She wished she could see the future.

It was then another plan came to her. The night was not over yet.

*　　　*　　　*

44

'Ewan, it was the safe thing to do.'

Ewan's mother had explained herself already a hundred times but it seemed her son would never understand. He sat with his arms folded, looking out the window.

'I am just annoyed that they sent us to this place,' she went on. 'This town is complete kip . . . and this house!'

She looked around the bare kitchen. They were sitting on the only two chairs. There was no table. The living room had no carpet. Even some of the bulbs were missing, their sockets hanging empty. The whole house was so empty it did not even contain smells. Homeliness had moved out and left no forwarding address.

'It feels strange to be in a house so abandoned and empty,' she said. 'It makes *me* feel abandoned and empty.'

Ewan glanced at his mother, too fast for her to notice. She did look empty, it was true. He looked out the window again. Ewan would rather be abandoned than feel like this. He felt they had abandoned his father. The house was grim, but they had enough money to furnish it and soon would. His father's cell would never have soft furnishings. His mother's testimony would help get his father freed, Ewan knew that, but in the meantime he was angry with her for separating them.

'We should not have run away,' he said.

'Some day you'll forgive me, Ewan. Deep down I think you know I did the right thing. I see how you march to and from school, with your head up. You're trying to look tough, like your father. But

45

you are not like him, I am glad you're not like him. Your strength is greater, it is in your intelligence.'

'Strength!' said Ewan, his coolness slipping. 'What does strength matter? Look at us. We've run away. We came here to hide.'

'Yes, we've run,' said his mother, a hint of pleading in her voice. 'I would've kept running if the ocean wasn't in the way. I am keeping us safe. This might be a horrible town but at least I know we'll be safe.'

'What is so great about being safe? Sometimes people have to take a stand.'

'It is not easy for either of us being here, I know that. We'll have trouble fitting in and just being happy. You want to take a stand? Then take it here, we have nowhere else to go. And I have a feeling things are going to get worse before they get better.'

Ewan stood.

'Where're you going?'

'I want to take a look around,' he said, 'I want to get to grips with this town.'

Ewan marched through the estate as if he was going somewhere important but in reality he had no idea where he was going. Near the town square he found the library and would have gone in but it was closed. From inside the town hall he heard the excited screams of the old ladies playing bingo. He did not want to go in there. Nor did he wish to go inside the Lobster's Cage. It radiated anger and adult rituals he would not understand for years, if ever. He passed it not long after May had moved on to her new destination. Ewan stopped marching and began wandering more slowly, studying the town as he went. He found the streets of Ballydog

46

mainly lifeless after dark. Here it was a darker dark than he was used to in the city, few cars went by and there were hardly any street lights. The brightest light source on one lane was the television set left on in the window of a shop closed for the night, 'Big Shocks Electricals'.

Having no television in his house, Ewan lingered to watch through the window. The world news was on. He could not hear the news reports but he enjoyed just being able to see pictures from the world beyond Ballydog. The newsreader was speaking to camera in the studio. The story title read: 'Unexplained Tremors in Atlantic'. A digital map of the southern Atlantic Ocean was shown with a red spot marked near the southern point of the Americas. Then a seismograph was shown, a continuous spool of graph paper running under a needle thin pen. It showed there had been an earthquake or tremor. Then the map was shown again and another spot marked. It was higher up than the first spot and about a thousand miles off the coast of Argentina. Then a third was marked. Next a few seconds of stock footage was shown: a military submarine cutting through rough seas. It was American. The last image of the report was the map again. There were three spots marked on it, they made a line heading north.

'Get away from there!' an angry voice shouted at him from a window above. 'Planning a burglary, are ya?'

Ewan decided not to argue. He set off back down the lane towards the estate and his house. He hoped his mother would have gone to bed by the time he got back.

CHAPTER NINE

May was on the wild side of town, the forgotten part where the streets ended and the countryside began. Carefully she picked her way along a lane known as the Batter; it was beyond the church, beyond the estate, beyond O'Hara's field. Hardly anybody ever came this way. Brambles, blackthorn bushes and nettles covered the ground, apart from where the path wound, while up above the branches of tall trees claimed the sky. It was dark here an hour before anywhere else in Ballydog and it took May a long time to find her way to the garden gate of the Woman on the Hill. May had not been frightened during the walk. Being alone in a forest at night did not trouble her. She might have been the only person alive in the whole world and part of her liked that feeling. She heard the disinterested *gerp-gerp* of frogs and felt the rustle of beetles going about their business. The girl passing through their patch did not bother them. They saw she was not a danger and accepted her without question. Here May was in harmony with her surroundings. Some night, she felt, she might say goodbye to everything, the whole cruel world, slip into the undergrowth and never come out.

May noticed that the animals along the lane were not frightened like the sea life had been the night before. It seemed not just the leatherback and crabs in the bay had left. The fleet had returned without fish. The sea around Ballydog was empty. Why had all the shoals of fish moved on? Because of the 'Big-Boss'? The Old Man of

48

the Sea was gone, May would get no more clues through him. Maybe the Woman on the Hill would understand. Maybe she could help.

The light from the two square windows of her cottage danced. It must have come from candles or oil burners. May paused and watched for a while, nervous of getting closer. The cottage belonged to fifty years ago, from long before May was born anyway. Apart from the television aerial on the chimney the house would have fitted in a fairy tale. The whole cottage was crooked and seemed half sunk back into nature. The garden was overgrown and wild, the path to the door broken up with weeds.

According to some of the old folk of Ballydog, the Woman on the Hill could read the future from the lines on a hand. It used to be that some folk would visit her late at night, although they would never admit it. In those days she lived with her son and his wife. The old woman was good at predicting the future, too good. Eventually amazement turned to fear and fear turned to hate. The secret visits stopped. Even her son and daughter-in-law left her. She was driven into the life of a hermit. Nobody had laid eyes on her in a long time, she was almost forgotten. The old woman never went down into Ballydog any more; she never even left her cottage. Once a week a man from the town picked up her pension cheque and brought her weekly supplies in two plastic bags from Kilfeather's shop. He left them outside her door and slipped away. Sometimes she would leave a note for him, asking for something extra the following week, but even he had not actually *seen* her in years, only her ancient handwriting across pieces of brown paper.

May was the first person in a long long time to knock on the old woman's front door. The sound of the knock hung in the air for a time after the physical act. It broke the evening stillness, so crude a noise that May shrank back. She thought about making a run for it.

From behind the door May heard a chair shift. Then there was silence. It was as if the old woman had pushed back in her chair, surprised at the knock, and was staring at the door wondering if she had imagined it. May tapped lightly on the door, as if to quietly say: *aye, it's true . . . someone has come to talk to ye*.

The chair shifted again. Footsteps moved towards the door, careful footsteps. Just where they should have stopped they made one more step. The door creaked against its frame. May realised the old woman was pressed right up against her door, listening probably.

'Who's out there?' a voice said through the door.

'It's only me, me name is May. I live here in Ballydog, I'm sorry to be knocking so late . . .'

Her words trailed off, what to say next?

'Oh, that's okay I suppose. Are ye lost?'

They both spoke in low voices but could hear each other fine. The door was between them but their faces were only centimetres apart. The old woman didn't seem to want to open it and something occurred to May. Nobody in Ballydog had seen the old woman in years but they were seeing each other every day, whereas in all that time the old woman had not seen a single living person. The people of Ballydog had turned against the Woman on the Hill and she was probably frightened of them. More, she was probably frightened of the whole rest of the world, everything beyond her front door.

'No, I'm not lost, I just wanna to speak to ye please, I'm fierce worried about something and I remember old folks down the town saying ye had an eye on the future, can ye help me please?'

There was a silence, the woman seemed to have drawn in her breath and held it there.

'I think ye should go on home now, me dear,' she said. 'The people of the town would only go mad if they knew I was putting ideas in the head of a youngster. They'd likely come up here and burn me out . . . Wouldn't be the first time such a thing happened in Ballydog.'

'No no, please, old lady, I won't tell them about coming up here,' said May, 'they won't care less anyway, I'm not exactly the darling of Ballydog meself. Is it true ye used to read palms?'

There was quiet again for a while and then the soft voice through the door saying, 'Aye it is, way back . . . It was a gift I would've given away if I could. Mainly a curse, to be honest.' She stopped. She was thinking, remembering. Then, 'Tell me, what's this thing you're worried about?'

The voice spoke in a kindly way that made May weak. She decided to explain her link with the animal kingdom first. She came out with it all there and then. It was a relief to speak so freely, her words poured out. She became almost frantic, her whisper urgent and breathless. The old woman was the first person May had ever met, if this could be called meeting, who she thought might actually understand. May's face was right up against the

51

door, she gave her secrets to it. She rarely spoke of these things to anybody and when she did they would look at her sadly and shake their heads. Or laugh. Her father became positively frightened when she brought up the subject of her link with animal life. He told her to try and stop it, that she was a victim of her own imagination. But that night, explaining herself to this . . . door, May realised something: even if nobody else believed her, she believed herself. *She* knew it was real. She had this link, this talent.

'That's quite a talent ye have there, me dear.'

May's heart leaped when she heard those words.

The old woman went on. 'Most people have a window on the spiritual plain, ye know. A link to God is what I think it is. Even ordinary people get the occasional omen here and there, a hunch that proves to be right, that kind of thing. They don't believe in magic or anything mad like that!'

The old woman let out a long dry laugh, she sounded like she smoked forty cigarettes a day.

'Anyways, other people have a bigger window, they can *see things*, me dear, *hear things*. Things that happened and sometimes things that are yet to be. These people, *our people*, me dear, get the picture in lots of different ways. Ye get it through God's creatures, that's original if ye don't mind me saying. As for this old woman, I get it from reading the lines in folk's hands. Or used to anyways. Years ago the people started fearing me and, to be honest, I got to be afeared of them. I shut me door and haven't laid eyes on a single human being in over ten years. Can ye believe that? It's not so bad. I used to miss going to the Mass on Sundays but not so much any more. Mass does be on the telly anyways.'

She let out another dry laugh.

'And now ye arrive wanting your palm read! What's the hurry to know the future I wonder? It'll be here upon us soon enough. Ye know ye have a gift, is that not plenty? It can be dangerous to know your future sometimes, because ye only ever get a glimpse and a glimpse alone can often mislead. Can ye not let the future alone 'til ye meet it?'

'Aye, but there is one thing I really need to know about,' said May. 'I'm sure it's important. There was this big leatherback turtle living here in the bay for a few months. He was me friend. He left last night and I got a warning from him, he said that we were all in trouble. A "Big-Boss" is coming, it's fierce angry with us and will swallow up the whole town. It sounds like mad-talk but could it be true?'

More silence. May did not attempt to hurry the woman. It would be the first time she had been asked to read a palm in years. Then there was a *tak* and a small patch of yellow light appeared on the path. The letter box in the middle of the door had snapped opened.

'All right, me dear, give me your hand then so,' the old woman said.

It took a few moments for May to grasp what the old woman was saying. She wanted May to put her hand through the letter box. The Woman on the Hill was not ready for the outside world yet. May felt her throat dry up, to give her hand over to someone she had never seen? It seemed dangerous, but she knew she had no option. Anything was better than the hollow sensation she

53

had been carrying around in her stomach for twenty-four hours now. The sensation that told her something was going to happen, something big. She had to learn all she could.

May knelt down on the front doorstep, gulped and put her right hand through the letter box. She felt as if she might never see it again. Then May experienced the sensation of the unseen woman's breath on her hand and the tips of her old fingers on her palm.

The woman examined her hand for a long time. She made little clicking noises and said a prayer. It would have been a strange scene to anyone who saw it; dark night, a girl kneeling at the door of a cottage, an expectant look on her face and her hand sticking in the letter box.

Then the voice behind the door spoke, 'The leatherback was a window, it cannot lie, this town will be destroyed and everyone in it will die.'

The old woman gave her prognosis in a matter-of-fact way but May's head reeled. The door, the cottage, the trees, all of Ballydog Bay and the whole wider world seemed to twist and go out of focus for a moment, then return sharply. She was numbed by the shock of the future. Ballydog was damned.

The woman continued, 'There is something else here and it feels important; I don't know what it means but I see a man will come down to ye from on high, he'll say that he wants to help ye but he will not. He'll put ye in danger for his own ends, do not trust him.'

Numbed, it took May a while to realise the old woman was no longer examining her hand, she was holding it. May did not feel trapped by this. She

54

felt comforted, shielded, for a little while at least. Then she realised something else, somebody was coming up the lane. It sounded like one person. It was dark, hopefully whoever it was would not notice her kneeing in the shadows at the end of the garden path and would pass by.

'What should I do?' whispered May. 'Is there anything I can do to stop it?'

'No. A furious hunger is awake and won't sleep 'til it's satisfied. It's not your fault and it's not your responsibility. This town chose its own fate.'

The footsteps on the lane were getting louder. Were they running? May thought so.

'There must be something that can be done?' whispered May. 'What about all the people? What about ye?' She squeezed the old woman's hand tightly. The woman squeezed hers in return.

'Me dear, such big worries for a young girl,' she said. 'Don't worry about me anyways, I always knew this house would be me tomb. I will pray for ye.'

May was listening to the old woman but was also watching the Batter. The man, it sounded like a man, would be passing the gate in seconds. May tried to make herself small against the door. There was too much happening at once: the prediction, the man running up the lane, the Big-Boss, the future approaching.

'But what should I do?' May demanded, her voice louder than she had meant it to be.

'There is nothing ye can do,' the old woman said.

The man saw May. He saw her immediately because she was the reason he was there. It was her dad. Some interfering person in the town had

55

probably seen May going up the Batter, went into the Lobster's Cage and told him.

'Come away from there, May,' he called. He was trying to sound light-hearted, as if May was doing something naughty that they would laugh about tomorrow. But there was real panic in his voice.

'This town chose its own fate—' the old woman was saying.

May's dad ran to the gate. May had never seen him run before. Her hand and the hand of the old woman were locked tight. May wished she could climb through the letter box, if only she was a bit smaller, please, please, please . . .

'But what should I do?' said May loudly.

Her father leaped the gate, ran up the path and tried to scoop her up in his arms. 'May, it's very late,' he said. He lifted and tugged her, but her hand was still in the letter box.

'But what should I do?' she demanded one last time at the door.

'Run away,' the old woman called, as their fingers slipped apart.

CHAPTER TEN

All the youngsters of the class were standing outside the school in a rabble, poking, spitting and laughing. Ewan was standing a bit away and looking around. May was not there that morning for some reason. The class was taking a walk to the lighthouse, an impromptu school tour. It was Heiferon's idea and he was going to bring them. Ballydog school tours were always bad, they never

56

even got to leave town. Once Heiferon brought them all to his house and made them pull out all the weeds in his garden. A 'botany field trip' he called it. Another time Heiferon led the class to the shore and had them collect bucketfuls of mussels. He sold them to a restaurant in the next town. 'That's business, boys and girls,' he had told them the next morning while waving the money at them, 'pure business.'

They set off. Heiferon was in the lead and singing at the top of his lungs. You would have thought they were marching to France rather than the few kilometres to the lighthouse.

Mr Weir lived in the lighthouse. He opened the door with a huge grin and seemed delighted to see them all.

'So you've come for a tour,' he said to Heiferon.

'That's right, say *thank you*, class.'

Some of the boys were a bit slow about it. Heiferon had to clout the backs of a few heads before they all said it.

Weir laughed at all this happening on his doorstep. 'I don't normally get visitors,' he said, 'and certainly not so many at once.'

Weir stepped aside and welcomed them in. Ewan was the last to enter and he examined Weir with interest. He had been expecting him to look like Captain Birds-Eye. To have a white beard and wear a blue cap. Weir did not look like that. He wore a black woollen pullover and had long grey hair instead of a beard. He was tall and thin like a mast. In fact he might have been the tallest person Ewan had ever seen in his life. His head almost reached the ceiling, and it was a high ceiling. There were deep lines on his face but he looked strong and fit. Ewan detected that Weir's friendliness was forced. His mouth was not really accustomed to smiling. Weir was exercising facial muscles today that he did not normally use.

'Most lighthouses,' Weir told the group, 'have a house or cottage nearby where the keeper lives. Not this one. I live in the tower itself, mainly up on the next floor. There is plenty of room because when they built this lighthouse they built it big. It is one of the biggest, and oldest, in the country.'

The ground floor was dedicated to the storage of boat parts and equipment. Ropes, pulleys, emergency flares and mechanical parts. There was no window in the circular room. A stone staircase went up to the next floor. Outside, the lighthouse was plastered and gleaming white, inside it could be seen that the tower was made of large grey blocks of stone. Everybody looked at the room in great detail. They had been seeing this lighthouse all their lives but none of them had ever been inside before. They asked Weir plenty of questions. They even experimented with being polite.

'It is a sturdy tower, for sure,' said Weir. 'I hope it will stand another hundred years and continue keeping Ballydog Bay safe.'

They all went up the stairs and through the trapdoor in a line. The next floor was the living quarters. The lighthouse tapered upwards, so this floor was slightly smaller than the first. It was packed with furniture, plants and books. The class barely squeezed in. There was a window, a kitchen area, a fold-down bed. On top of a workbench was something round-shaped, concealed by a sheet. On the stove a covered pot was steaming and producing a rich chocolate smell. Everybody noticed it and felt hungry. Everyone also noticed the pictures stuck up on the walls with Blu-tack. They were drawn with charcoal, presumably by Mr Weir himself, and were views from the lighthouse. The mouth of the bay was what Weir liked to draw most.

'Drawing is my hobby,' said Weir, and the class were impressed.

The class had never been so well behaved. They were not like a Ballydog class at all. Heiferon was not liking it, they never listened to *him* so closely, or said 'please, sir' before they asked him a question.

Weir clapped his hands together. 'Let's see what's cooking, shall we?'

A few moments later each of the class was eating Dim Sum from the pot on the stove. Dim Sum were steamed bread rolls and these had chocolate sauce in the middle. As their teeth sank into the dough more of the rich smell was released. For a while there was quiet, apart from the sounds of enjoyment from the class.

'That there is what they have for breakfast in Hong Kong,' said Weir. 'I was a ship's cook as a younger man, learned to make all manner of foreign delicacies.'

Everyone was licking their fingers. Weir's popularity was established with most of the class.

'How do you make—' a boy began to ask but Heiferon interrupted.

'What's that for?' He was pointing at a white steel box attached to the wall. It had a door in it and a small glass panel. Inside lit-up buttons glimmered red and green. A thick cable ran from it along the wall and up through the roof. The sharper students in the class realised Heiferon already knew what it was. If he did not then he would not have asked. Heiferon would never draw attention to a lack of knowledge on his part. If he ever asked a question he was only asking as part of a trick or game designed, like his mousetraps, for cruelty.

Sure enough the question made Weir uncomfortable. 'Oh, that thing . . . it's not very interesting for young ones.' He waved his hand at it dismissively. 'That's a gadget the Lighthouse Commission installed to help me take care of the bay.'

'Really?' said Heiferon. 'Amazing the technology they have these days, isn't it? The light is automated, is it? All the work done for you. No wonder you have all that time to draw.'

'Are we done?' said Weir, looking at the students. 'Up we go to my study and then, if you promise to be careful, we can go up, four at a time, to the top platform and look at the light itself.'

Now that *was* exciting. A ripple of anticipation ran through the class.

The next room was almost empty, just a chair and a table and a ladder going to the next level. It looked like a room for thinking. The window faced towards the mouth of the bay. Several trawlers could be seen returning to port. This was hours earlier than usual, probably another bad day's fishing. Members of the class jostled around the window trying to get a look. In contrast Weir had to bow in order to see out.

'I can't see which boats they are,' said one of the boys. 'They're still too far away.'

Weir looked around the class. 'Could you pop

60

back downstairs and get my binoculars, son?' he asked a boy. 'They're on my workbench, I believe.'

Ewan went to do as he was asked.

'Andrew!' barked Heiferon. 'You go with him. Never trust a Northerner, they have criminality in their bones.'

They went downstairs. Andrew was sour about it and stopped before he was at the bottom of the steps. He leaned against the wall and put his hands in his pockets. Ewan went over to the bench. As he picked up the binoculars he looked at the large covered object that was sitting on the bench. He was curious, Ewan was the kind of boy who always had to *know*. He lifted the corner of the sheet and looked underneath but was still no wiser as to what the object actually was. It was shaped like a giant light bulb, but of shiny steel, not glass. It had a spherical section, open at the base, and a metre-long funnel soldered to it.

'Being as we're being nosy,' said Andrew, 'let's do it right.'

He jumped off the stairs and began poking about the room. At first Ewan was happy to be included in something Andrew wanted to do. Then it dawned on him that Andrew's intension was to steal something. He was opening cupboards and drawers, making a quick search.

Ewan dropped the corner of the sheet. 'I was only looking,' he said.

'Shut it, I'm busy,' hissed Andrew. He flitted from one place to another, checking everything but leaving it all exactly as he found it. He wanted something to show to the pack later in The Villa. It was not important what he stole, it did not have to be valuable, but he did not want something worthless either. Upstairs they could hear Weir talking to the class and Heiferon butting in whenever he could. They were not missing the boys or the binoculars yet.

Andrew pulled open the top drawer of a large chest of drawers. It was not a normal chest of drawers like for putting clothes in. It was low, with drawers only six or seven centimetres high but extremely wide. Ewan had never seen a piece of furniture like it before but he was sure it was for storing charts and maps out flat, without having to put folds in them. He was right, but Weir was storing more than just charts.

Andrew jumped back as if he had found a live snake in there. Then he stared into the drawer with a disbelieving expression.

'Impossible,' he said.

Ewan went over to see what had caused this reaction.

Mr Weir was storing charcoal drawings in the chest. The drawing on top, the one that Andrew was staring at, was of a sea creature. It was long and huge. It stood out of the waves. Uncountable legs stuck from its body. Its eyes were on stalks, they were vacant and empty. Its face was all mouth. From its throat sprang fifty tongues.

*　　　*　　　*

'Thank you, son,' Weir said as Ewan handed him the binoculars, but the group were no longer interested in the view. Weir was telling stories and explaining the workings of the light. The class were standing in a crescent moon shape around him and listening intently to every word. Ewan stayed near to Weir. He wanted to get a good look at this lighthouse keeper. How did he and Andrew both come to draw the same thing independently of each other? Had Weir produced it in a trance too?

Andrew sat at the top of the stairs. He looked ill.

Weir had warmed up to his role as tour guide. He told stories of the Spanish Armada, German U-boats of the Second World War and Ballydog trawlers that were smashed on the rocks of the bay. He kept returning to the same theme, it was his job to 'take care of the bay'. It seemed to be his obsession, but the group did not mind listening to him going on about it. Such passion was rare in Ballydog, unless it was a passion for badness. He used his hands expressively as he spoke. He reminded Ewan of some of the evangelical ministers he had seen on the streets of his city. A *missionary zeal* was what Weir's type of energy was called.

'Speaking of boats,' he said, 'I have a neighbour who is in this class, I believe. The girl who lives on the *Sunny Buoy* down at the old quay. Which of you is she?'

Heiferon snorted. 'You're out of luck, this is the morning she spends with her head-doctor. We left her behind.'

Weir's hands dropped. 'That is unfortunate,' he said. 'I see her on deck sometimes when I pass but I have never met her.'

'She suffers from an overactive imagination,' said Heiferon. 'She hears voices in her head. Thinks animals tell her things. Soft in the head she is.' Heiferon made the international hand signal for insanity: pointed his finger at the side of his head and revolved it in a small circle. He laughed and most of the class sniggered along with him.

'Well,' said Weir, offended. 'I have heard of stranger things. I believe there is more in this world than any one of us can understand.'

Heiferon's chest filled up like a sail. 'Get a grip,' he bellowed, 'don't be putting nonsense like that in these youngsters' heads. She is soft in the head and that's that.'

'You don't have to like it,' said Weir, 'but it's what I believe. There is more to humanity than even a teacher is going to understand, Mr Heiferon.'

Heiferon made a succession of flustered and disgusted noises, none of which came close to forming a word. Then he managed to say, 'Come on, class, we're going. This man is a bad influence.'

The class were disappointed. They had all been looking forward to climbing up top to the light. The ladder was right there between them, it led to a trapdoor in the roof. The class looked from one man to the other, hoping they might work it out, but Weir did not care to make amends.

'Yes,' said Weir, 'tour over.'

Heiferon herded the class back down the stairs. Ewan delayed and watched Weir. He was sure Weir had lost interest in his visitors as soon as he learned May was not among them. As if to confirm this suspicion Weir followed the class down, took the last Dim Sum out of the pot and wrapped it in drawing paper for May. He gave it to one of the girls, a particularly spiteful one whose name Ewan did not know nor wanted to, and asked her to give it to 'the girl who lives on the boat'. Ewan was surprised by the lighthouse keeper's innocence.

Even Ewan knew, and it did not matter *which* of the class Weir asked to pass on the Dim Sum, that May would not taste one crumb of it. Weir should have given it to him.

Heiferon huffed as he led the class back towards school. The students would not stop babbling about the lighthouse and Mr Weir. They had all found the lighthouse keeper exciting and enigmatic. Heiferon could stand it no longer. He stopped and turned on them. He began ranting.

'Sorry to break your hearts, but the only reason the Lighthouse Commission let Weir stay there is because they know he has nowhere else to go. Him going on about *keeping the bay safe* is ridiculous. It's all automatic, it switches itself on and off. He has been unemployed for years. Some day they'll probably toss him out on his ear. He's only a liability, if you ask me. He obviously just spends day and night walking up and down those stairs developing *the quare ways*. He has no purpose any more.'

Satisfied, Heiferon turned and began marching again. The class were sad to hear this news about Mr Weir, but it was bad news, so they knew it was true.

CHAPTER ELEVEN

After the belch of the intercom marked the beginning of break the children of Ballydog Secondary migrated to the schoolyard and spread out over it. Andrew and his pack went to their place, behind the boiler house. It was a cramped alley, with layers of soft drink cans on the ground, many so old they had turned white. The unpleasant smell of oil came from the boiler house and there was a diesel warmth thick in the air. The pack all smoked cigarettes, except for Tonne MacPherson who was grunting and crushing cans under his slab-like feet. Andrew was leaning against the wall, feeling the vibrations of the machines in the boiler house. He was not speaking to anyone. He was in a bad mood.

'Hello, boys,' said Cynthia, as she came around the corner, 'your hidey-hole sure stinks.' She went to kick a can but then thought better of it. She did not want to dirty her shoes.

The boys did not know how to act. She had never been there before, no girl ever had. She pulled out a cigarette and the boys fought to be the one to light it. She accepted a light from Mushroom. He grinned with satisfaction. Andrew noticed all this but chose not to involve himself. He had bigger worries.

There were a hundred explanations as to how he and Weir, that weirdo, had made the same drawing. It was probably in some movie they had both seen, or in some stupid comic. He only wished that Northboy hadn't seen both drawings too, if it wasn't for that he could easily forget about it, deny it and make it go away. But now it was like Northboy had something on him, a powerful piece of information he could use to make Andrew seem like a weirdo too. Northboy had seen the way Andrew had lost control of himself and drawn that . . . thing. Andrew rubbed his forehead. He had not slept properly the night before either, it was that dream again.

He is standing at the end of a pier, he knows he could run but he does not. He sees the creature under the water . . . it is bigger than the bay —

Andrew snapped out of it. *Only a dream*, he told himself, and looked around at the pack. They would turn on him the second they got a sniff of weakness.

Then he saw May.

May kept her hands held behind her back so the pack would not see she was shaking. They grinned at her and their grins were like snarls. She was surprised to see Cynthia but looked immediately for Andrew. He was at the back, the gang were like his bodyguards.

'Andrew, can I speak to ye for a minute, please?' May asked.

Cynthia was leaning against the wall with Mushroom. 'Whooo, Andrew,' she said, 'is this your girlfriend now?'

If one of the boys had said that, Andrew would have told him to *shut it*. As it was Cynthia he did not know how to react.

'Yeah, are you and May going together now, Andrew?' one of the boys laughed.

'Shut it,' said Andrew. He leaned back against the wall and looked up at the sky. He took a drag of his cigarette. He did not look at May.

'Andrew, can I speak to ye for a minute, please?' May repeated.

Andrew made a bored sigh and, still looking at the sky: 'Fire away then, go on.'

May glanced nervously from side to side and said, 'Maybe in private?'

The pack's laughter was loud and unnaturally long. Even MacPherson managed to produce

67

laugh-type noises. 'She wants a private session,' they squealed. 'Mind yourself, Andrew.' When they had settled down, Andrew said what he knew he had to say if he was to keep his position with the pack.

'You can say whatever you want to say in front of all of us, go on.'

Andrew always knew what his gang wanted and now they wanted to laugh at May. His hands were tied. He could not try to take this laugh away from them because they would probably ignore him and laugh at May anyway. Then his status would have sunk.

'What do you want to ask him?' said Mushroom.

May spoke directly to Andrew, 'I want ye to help me fix up the engine of the *Sunny Buoy*, I wanna get it running again.' May raised her hands, her palms were the colour of rust and streaked with grease. 'I've been trying but I don't know how . . .'

The pack was disappointed. This was actually a sensible thing to ask Andrew. Not a weirdo request at all. Andrew was a good mechanic. He even knew how to drive. If you had a technical question, you asked Andrew, it made sense.

But Andrew did not want to help. He was not even looking at her.

'I could get a bit of money for ye, maybe?' said May.

'Charge her all her pocket money for the rest of the year,' said one of the boys.

'Sure, she gets no pocket money,' said another. 'Her dad spends it all on drink.'

'Why do you want to get the boat running, going fishing?' Mushroom asked. He was losing

68

patience; he wanted a laugh, not a conversation with this oddball.

'I wanna be able to leave town on it if I have to, and bring me dad,' said May. She directed her words to Andrew and nobody else. 'Ye can come too, Andrew, if ye help me.'

That made Andrew look at last. 'Why would we want to leave?' he asked her.

'I think something big is goin' to happen to Ballydog, I don't wanna to be here when it does,' said May.

Andrew could not stop himself. He pulled himself from the wall and stepped towards May. The eyes of the pack turned on him. He could feel the fear in May and he had the same fear. Something big was going to happen. She was right.

May saw the flicker of understanding cross his face. Just for a second but definitely there. 'Please, Andrew, I can't do it by meself, something terrible is coming. A Big-Boss.'

'A "Big-Boss"?' sneered Cynthia.

Andrew's mind was reeling. He felt his legs become weak beneath him. The boiler house rumbled. It was like a storm brewing.

'What's a "Big-Boss", what's that?' Mushroom demanded. 'Who told you about it?'

The pack were frustrated. They just wanted a laugh, instead everything was turning serious. They looked to Andrew to save the situation. Andrew tore his eyes away from May's pleading face and looked at his pack. He hesitated.

'Who told you about it?' said Mushroom. The other boys joined in. May was shaking visibly.

'Quiet, lads, back off her,' Andrew said. It worked, they shut their gobs. Andrew paused and

69

looked at her. He stepped closer. He put his hands on her shoulders to help her stop shaking.

'Tell me, May, who told you about a Big-Boss? I need to know before I can help you.'

May turned to putty in his hands, she might have fallen over if he had not been holding her upright. 'Ye'll think I'm crazy, but it was an old turtle,' she told him quietly. 'He was living at the old pier with me for a few months.'

Everything went quiet. For a few long moments Andrew considered.

'May,' he said with slow gravity, 'I don't think you're crazy . . . I *know* you're crazy. Now why don't you run back out to the yard and have a chat with the seagulls, maybe they can help you.'

The pack collapsed in laughter.

'Or the sheep in the fields!' they said. 'Or the dogs in the street!'

That was one reason Andrew was boss, he supplied jokes so well. He had the admiration of all the pack. Yet Andrew himself did not laugh, he was just relieved the whole scene was over. When he turned his back, May ran away.

CHAPTER TWELVE

Ewan descended the stairs to the library. He shivered, it was chilly down there.

Ballydog Library had a good selection of bad books and a bad selection of good ones. It only opened after dark and nobody was really sure when it closed. It was in the basement of one of the town's oldest buildings. The library was lit by a

70

single forty-watt bulb and it was hard to make out the titles on the shelves that lined the four walls. There was a desk in the middle of the room and on it was something that Ewan was both surprised and happy to see: a computer with an internet connection. At the time the librarian herself was on the computer. Her long white fingers working the keyboard were the only part of her that moved. The computer screen was reflected in her large eyes. The sound of her typing was a continuous crackling, like twigs breaking. She was dressed in black and had black hair, but her skin was extremely pale. If you stayed in this dark library and looked upon her for long enough then you might start to forget that colours existed. All the colours might have drained from your mind.

'Excuse me,' said Ewan. Miss Cancer looked up at him. Her fingers remained frozen over the keyboard. She was young, the skin of her face was as white and smooth as a plate, and perhaps as cold. She did not say a word but looked at Ewan through her wide unblinking eyes.

'Can you help me? I'm looking for books on mythical creatures.'

She opened the library catalogue on the computer and looked for books on that subject.

'We have some . . .' she said, after a lengthy pause. Her voice was low but she had a Ballydog accent. 'But Mr Weir, the lighthouse keeper, has borrowed them all. In fact, they are overdue.' She looked at Ewan again and said, 'I shall have to send him a letter.'

'Okay. Well, thanks. Thank you anyway,' said Ewan. She made him nervous. 'I'll go have a look what's here.'

71

Ewan walked along the shelves. There were wide gaps between books and Ewan wondered if the librarian's letters were as effective as they might have been. Still, it gave Ewan real pleasure to run his fingers along the spines of the books. He was glad to be in a library. The library had been his favourite place in the city. From there he had connected with the rest of the world. He liked being in the company of knowledge, he realised. Even bad knowledge would do.

In a book called 'Ways to Frighten Your Children', Ewan found a chapter on monsters. It discussed their purposes: a dragon's purpose was to kidnap princesses; banshees howled on the night of a death. This was all very interesting, but Ewan could find nothing that sounded like the creature in Andrew's and Weir's drawings. There was nothing that hinted at *its* purpose.

It was not as hard as he had predicted to persuade the librarian to let him use the internet. He asked for just half an hour and she rose out of her seat silently. Ewan sat down and found the seat strangely cold. First he looked at a few news websites, quickly scanning the headlines. There had been other unexplained seismological events in the Atlantic over the last few days, away from known fault lines. Under the headline 'Submarine on the Prowl?' a general of the US navy was questioned about alleged sightings of one of their submarines, the *Deep Trouble*, in the area. He was denying it. Scientists were debating the possible causes of the tremors but it was not a big news story, there was no threat to human life, nobody was too concerned. Ewan made a note of all this in his pocket notebook.

Then he did a search. He tried 'Sea+ monster+real' then 'Creature+undiscovered+ Ballydog' and then 'Monster+sea+Ballydog'. All he was having returned to him was pages about movies and computer games and the search engine was refusing to believe that 'Ballydog' was a real word at all. Ewan kept searching; it felt important to keep searching but he was becoming sure that if he was to get real answers he would have to get Andrew on side. That would not be easy. He would also have to speak to May. During the day he had heard Andrew's pack saying she had told them something big was going to happen to Ballydog. They were laughing about her, of course, but they had not seemed able to drop the subject. It was as if her words had hit a nerve.

He kept looking. His searches were starting to look like a strange maths problem. Sea + creature + Ballydog = something bad.

As the librarian hovered around the shelves, tidying the books, Ewan scanned page after page. The words: 'Having a problem with an unheard-of-creature?' made Ewan stop and read one webpage.

It was the website of Alexander Bam Brilski Teodors, Monster Hunter. It was in seven languages, with English as one of the options. There were no pictures. The text said he was available for contract and had a ninety-eight per cent success rate. Over forty dead creatures to his name. He promised full discretion: 'None of my exterminations have ever made it into the media,' he wrote. He had been in the Russian army for ten years before becoming a freelance monster hunter. Typical commissions for him were 'unlisted creatures' discovered in deep mines or remote

73

areas. Jungle clearance before the building of tourist resorts was a major employer for him. He listed the 'systems and tools' he was expert in, these included marksmanship and the deployment of tactical explosives. He was 'quite good' at karate.

One claim really stood out. Teodors had flying equipment, powered by 'the plasma of a fire-breathing salamander'.

Only a couple of days before Ewan might have thought this website was a joke. Now he was not so sure. He clicked on 'contact me' and typed Mr Teodors a message. He gave his first name and the whereabouts of Ballydog. He described the monster from the drawings and asked the monster hunter if he had ever heard of such a creature. Could it be real? Did he have any advice? Then he wrote 'thank you' and 'goodbye' and clicked 'send'. He wondered if he would ever get an e-mail from this Teodors person. He didn't think it very likely.

Ewan left the library but did not go back to his house. He had somewhere else to go.

CHAPTER THIRTEEN

Andrew was watching the odd behaviour of the pack's pet goldfish, Finn. Finn lived in a glass bowl filled with rainwater. It was sitting on a crate in front of Andrew's throne. Andrew had never seen it, or any fish, act so strangely. It was swimming in circles as usual but after each circle it rammed the inside of the bowl with its head, hard. The small thump could probably be heard right across The

74

Villa if the rest of the pack were not talking, fighting and generally making a racket. Then the goldfish would recover, swim another circle and do it again. It had been doing it all evening. It was as if Finn wanted to smash its way out. It was very weird. The little fish did not have a chance of making even a tiny crack in the glass. And what would it do if it did? Yet it continued ramming the inside of the bowl with its head, driven by an urge beyond Andrew's senses.

Andrew looked up. Ewan was standing there, looking down at him calmly. The pack had been so intent on their messing and Andrew had been watching Finn so closely that none of them had noticed Ewan walk right in. The fright of Ewan's sudden appearance made Andrew sink down in his chair.

'What's wrong with the fish?' asked Ewan.

At the sound of his voice the boys leaped to attention. Him! Here! Time to sort him out. They closed in. Andrew put his hands behind his head, to appear casual.

'Who invited you?' he said.

'I did,' answered Ewan.

'Thought so, well you can turn around and head straight back out. Keep walking until you are back in the North. Nobody wants you here.'

'Perhaps I can ask you a favour first?' said Ewan.

Andrew groaned. First May and now Northboy, both wanting to pull him somewhere he did not want to go. The bad dreams were doing the same thing, he knew it, dragging him down to a dark place. The dreams were getting so bad he was frightened to go to sleep.

'I'm not one bit frightened,' Andrew blurted at Ewan. His pack did not know what he was referring to and looked at him quizzically.

'Why you even talking to this weirdo anyway, Andrew?' said one of the boys. 'Let's show him how we do things here.' They were moving in and around Ewan. Tonne MacPherson was grunting excitedly.

'It is nothing to do with being frightened, Andrew,' said Ewan. 'But something very strange has happened, you know what, and I think we should investigate. I am asking you to visit Mr Weir with me.'

'What right have you got to be coming into The Villa and making requests?' said Mushroom. 'You have to be tested just to come in here, you've earned no right.'

'Yeah,' a couple of the boys agreed. 'Let's give Northboy a test, will we, Andrew?'

'Wouldn't matter if he passed,' said Andrew, 'he's not joining The Villa, not now, not ever.'

'I have no desire to be in your gang,' said Ewan. The boys were insulted and mystified at the same time. A boy not wanting to be in the pack was inconceivable to them.

'Then let's test him to see if he should be allowed to leave . . .' said Mushroom, 'with all his teeth.'

The pack used tests for all sorts of things. Joining, staying-in and being suspected of weakness or some other crime against The Villa would lead to a test. It was always Andrew who decided which test to use. Playing backgammon against Mushroom had been a test. Andrew stopped using it when he got sick of listening to

76

Mushroom's gloating commentary as he took the lead and won. Backgammon was a danger-free test compared to most of them. In 'Running the rooftops' for example, the boy had to get from one side of the estate to the other without touching the ground. They had to walk narrow walls, leap from roof to roof and swing along the branches of trees as they travelled. They usually did touch the ground before making it across the estate. They usually touched it hard.

'Let's see how he gets on with MacPherson,' one boy yelled, a childish bloodlust in his voice.

Fighting Tonne MacPherson was a popular test, especially with Tonne himself. It was a test nobody ever passed. Tonne lumbered over to the Northboy. His thick arms and fists swung like pendulums. Ewan looked up at him and felt his composure slip. Tonne was bigger than any boy in the school and a clear foot-and-a-half taller than Ewan. If it came to a fight he would have no chance. Tonne would never back off, he would have to be pulled off. Tonne's thick lips parted in a kind of smile and Ewan saw that his teeth were so coated in plaque you could not tell where one tooth ended and the next one began. His breath alone was nearly enough to knock Ewan over. Tonne was a blunt instrument on legs.

'Scrap, scrap!' a boy screamed.

'Shut it!' Andrew yelled at the boy, half out of his seat. 'I'm the one to decide that. I'm sick of looking at him. I just want him outta here, right now. There'll be no testing and I'm not going to any lighthouse.'

The boy who had screamed put on a sour look. MacPherson whined when it finally dawned on him

77

that he was not going to be allowed to beat up the Northboy.

'Waannn cak bee op,' he complained. MacPherson was hard to understand. He was led away by a couple of the other boys. There was an ugly sense of disappointment in the air. Ewan decided it was best to say nothing.

'I've got a better idea,' said Mushroom with a wicked gleam in his eye, 'a little test, why not? We owe it to William to get his watch back.'

The words seemed innocent enough to Ewan but he detected a strong reaction pass through the pack as soon as Mushroom uttered them. It was a ripple of energy somewhere between disgust and excitement, like a serious rule had been broken. There was a long pause and then murmurs of agreement.

'Yeah.'

'Good idea.'

A tension came over The Villa.

'I already said no,' repeated Andrew.

Andrew thought about whether he should stand up now or remain in his seat. Would standing help the situation or would it only take it further out of his control?

'Come on, Andrew,' said a few of the boys. 'Why not?'

'Yeah, Andrew,' prodded Mushroom, his eyes narrowed. 'Let's go with my idea.'

So this had become a leadership challenge. Mushroom was moving in and Andrew had to stop him. He could not let Mushroom's idea win, that would mean he had lost and everyone would know it. Andrew had to do something now or tomorrow night Mushroom would be sitting on his seat and

78

ruling The Villa. Andrew had already caught him testing the springs a couple of times.

'Do you all not remember what happened to William?' Andrew asked the pack. He realised immediately his mistake. He had spoken to all of them instead of just Mushroom, he had already shown that this was a power struggle, an election. And there had been pleading in his voice. A pack can smell fear.

Who is William? thought Ewan.

'That won't happen to Northboy,' said Mushroom. 'William was a fatso, Northboy will be faster on his feet.'

'I don't care, no,' said Andrew.

'It's the decent thing to do, isn't it, lads? We could post it to him.' Mushroom had turned his back on Andrew and was facing the gang.

'Yeah,' they agreed.

Andrew looked at Mushroom, where would be the best place to hurt him? Maybe if he could bring Mushroom down, right now and quickly, he could hold his leadership. But what side would the gang take if it came to a fight? Would they attack Andrew if he attacked Mushroom? Even if only Tonne defended Mushroom that would be enough to make Andrew the loser. There was a definite risk that Tonne would take Mushroom's side. Andrew had just denied him a scrap and besides, Tonne and Mushroom were always hanging around together these days. The brain and the brawn had combined and were dangerous.

Then Ewan spoke. He spoke to Andrew.

'Andrew, can I make you a deal? I will get William's watch back for you if you'll then grant me my favour. What do you think?'

79

With those words the atmosphere defused.

Andrew leaned back in his chair and everybody looked at him, even Mushroom. The attention of The Villa was focused back on Andrew again and he calmed down. In an odd way Ewan had just saved Andrew, he had asked *him* to make a deal, respected *him*. Now the whole Villa could only wait for Andrew's decision. Andrew was boss. He let the moment stretch longer than he had to. The only sound was the low thump of the goldfish banging its head against the inside of the bowl.

'Okay, Northboy, I think you're crazy but if that is what you want I'll do that deal with you,' Andrew said. 'Good luck . . . You'll need it.' Then he yawned, Andrew was good at faking boredom, and said, 'I want nothing to do with it. I'm going home. Mushroom, you take him to O'Hara's field.'

*   *   *

'William wanted to join The Villa. We were against it. His father is the bank manager but we are all estaters. Come to think of it,' said Mushroom, 'William was all polite and a bit snobby like you. But he still wasn't half as stiff as you.'

Ewan ignored that comment.

Mushroom was talking to Ewan as they walked through the dark forest. Behind them, Tonne was lumbering along and behind him other gang members were carrying a long ladder. The breathing of the convoy was making clouds of condensation in the cold air.

'William's folks had stacks of money and he had some kind of fancy watch that cost a fortune. We told him he would have to sacrifice his watch to

80

The Villa if he wanted to join. He nearly started crying there and then but sure enough he took the watch off and went to hand it over to Andrew. We didn't expect that,' Mushroom laughed. 'Naw, we said. You have to present it to our mascot in O'Hara's field.'

Ahead of them, out of the night, a shape was emerging. An old stone wall, almost as tall as the trees. To the right and left it disappeared into darkness. Ewan now knew what the ladder was for.

While the boys placed the ladder against the wall, Mushroom went on, 'This is O'Hara's field; apart from the gate, which is always locked, it is completely surrounded by this wall. They say it was built in famine times, when a good crop had to be guarded. Only grass grows in there now. At the top end of the field lives O'Hara's bull. Right now it'll be asleep. It's tied up and kept to a circular patch about twenty-five metres in diameter. I'm telling you this so you know that when you drop into the field you'll still be safe. The bull is at the far end and can't touch you even if it does wake up. Still, be nice and quiet because for your test you have to go into the danger zone.'

Ewan had expected something like that.

'This is one angry bull,' said Mushroom, the evil glint in his eye just about visible in the black silhouette of his head. 'If it wakes up it'll skewer you with its horns, like a marshmallow at a campfire. Your only hope will be to get out of its range *fast*. Bring us back William's watch and you pass.'

'Where exactly is the watch?' Ewan asked.

'Where do you think, Northboy?' said Mushroom. 'Strapped to one of its horns. It was

81

William's test to put it there.' Tonne produced a laugh-noise.

Ewan's heart rate went up. 'So he succeeded then, this William?'

'Depends how you look at it,' said Mushroom, managing to sound thoughtful. 'He got the watch on the bull's horn but then it woke up and trampled him. He spent three weeks in a coma and now he's in some sort of special school in Sligo.'

From the top of the ladder, Ewan looked out across O'Hara's field. There was hardly an ounce of light in the air but he knew that somewhere in the gloom the bull was sleeping.

'Stop daydreaming and get off the ladder,' hissed Mushroom from beneath him. 'Sit on the wall till we get up as well.'

The wall was narrow as well as high. Ewan slid himself along it. Mushroom sat beside Ewan and finally MacPherson pulled himself up and awkwardly placed himself on the other side of the ladder. Then Mushroom and MacPherson raised the ladder and quietly lowered it down the other side. The other boys waited outside the wall, it was too dark to see anything from the top anyway.

'Ga wa,' said MacPherson.

'You heard him, off you go,' said Mushroom.

Carefully, Ewan descended. The squeak of the ladder under his shoes seemed dangerously loud in the still night. As one foot then the other settled on the grassy field he felt his adrenalin pick up. He focused to slow his breathing; it was too fast and too loud. The clouds of his breath made him feel like a steam train. Directly ahead of him there was nothing but pitch-blackness. He started moving into it and the darkness wrapped around him.

82

After thirty metres or so he looked back, there was a little light in the air above Ballydog and it created a silhouette of the wall and the treetops beyond. He could see the outline of MacPherson and Mushroom sitting on the wall waiting for him. He faced back into the black and continued. Another twenty metres and he knew he was close to the bull, the ground sharply went from flat and grassy to a churned mess of mud. He had crossed into the danger zone. The destroyed ground made Ewan want to meet the bull even less, it obviously had a temper. Further, and the air became warm.

Ewan had found it. He could make out a faint glint coming from the thick metal ring in its nose. Its mass loomed out of the darkness as he approached, one tonne of meat and muscle. Its backbone arched up above Ewan's height and swept down to its small thick-skulled head tucked in against the ground. It was asleep. Its horns formed a shape like a crescent moon and made Ewan gulp. Around its neck was a thick collar of leather and bolts, designed never to be removed. A thick rope ran from it to a post hammered into the ground. He could hear the bull, see the bull, but he could actually feel it as well. It was generating a meaty warmth that Ewan could sense on his skin two metres away. A thought occurred to him: it was strange that the people of Ballydog would refuse to believe in monsters when this thing lived so close to their homes. Monsters, he reasoned, must cease to be monsters when you see them everyday.

Just get on with it, he told himself, *this is no time for philosophy*.

William's watch was on the left horn, all the way

down to where it protruded from the creature's skull. It was battered and coated in muck. It would never tell the correct time again. Still, it was tonight's top prize.

Ewan compared two possible plans. Plan A was to go slow, reach out and delicately take hold of the watch between his thumb and forefinger. Then slowly and quietly slide it back up along the horn until it was his. Then creep out of the bull's range.

Plan B was to do all the same things but without caution. Just do it fast. The bull was bound to wake, but hopefully Ewan would be out of its range by the time it reacted.

Ewan chose plan A, slow and careful was more his style. He reached out and positioned his finger and thumb around the watch. He held his breath and lightly touched it. Instantly the bull's breath was cut short, two angry blasts of condensation shot from its nostrils and its eyes flicked open. Ewan looked at the bull. The bull looked at Ewan.

Ewan switched to plan B.

He leaped at it, a foolhardy move nobody had ever pulled on this creature before. The bull swung its head away as it raised itself off the ground, but that was an advantage to Ewan. He was on the best side of the creature to grab the watch. He pulled it over the horn but now he was in a bad position, virtually on top of the angry animal. The bull's legs shot straighter than straight. It bucked, all four of its hooves leaving the ground for an instant. Ewan was thrown up in the air and, as he sailed upward, time seemed to slow down. He had time to wonder if those two horns would be waiting to catch him on his return to earth.

He hit the mud. Next he was trying to stand and

run in the same moment. The bull snorted and prepared to charge. Ewan ran and one tonne of rage thundered after him.

Instinct drove Ewan as much as it drove the bull. It was like being chased by an avalanche. Once he reached the grass, beyond the bull's range, he would be safe.

The grass, the grass.

The thought of the grass fuelled him. As he ran he imagined the texture of grass, he longed for it, it would be like heaven. Suddenly he was flying through the air and had grass in his teeth. He had been tripped by the edge of the bull's patch. He pulled himself up but now felt safe. The bull could not reach him there. He looked back, unable to resist seeing the bull's charge cut short. At the same instant the bull tore, full speed, out of the night towards the edge of its range.

Four things happened, one after another but all in the same few seconds.

The bull was stopped, it yelped as its collar snapped it back.

Ewan heard a *swwwwwwish* followed by the thump of something striking the ground.

Ewan realised what these sounds were. The rope had been snapped by the bull's momentum, and had swung through the air and hit the ground. The bull was free.

Then the bull realised it was free.

Oh no.

Ewan ran so hard his breath burned, he was aware only of his direction and the shaking earth. If he tripped again the charging bull would trample him into the ground. He could see the silhouettes of Mushroom and MacPherson on the wall ahead

85

of him and aimed himself between them.

Pull me up! Pull me up! Ewan desperately hoped they would begin to pull up the ladder up as soon as he was on it, maybe even before he was on it. He was going to need every fraction of a second. *Start taking up the ladder*, he wanted to scream but could not spare the breath. Where had MacPherson gone? Ewan could no longer see him on the wall.

Just twenty metres to go.

Behind him the bull was like a rock rolling down a mountain.

The ladder! The ladder!

Just ten.

What?

They had already pulled up the ladder. It was gone.

'So you did come back,' Mushroom said from above. 'We got bored and decided to go home. Sorry.'

Mushroom slipped out of view. He was climbing down the ladder on the other side of the wall.

Ewan turned to meet his fate. The ground beneath his feet was shaking. Bits of mortar in the stonework behind him were breaking loose and falling.

Need plan . . . Plan.

Got one. He would step aside at the last possible moment, the bull would charge into the wall. It was an old wall and Ewan, in the split second he had to think about the plan, thought there was a chance the animal would smash a hole in it. Then he would be able to get out of the field and climb a tree maybe. But hang on, how come it had not arrived yet? The shudders in the ground were less powerful now, and further apart. The creature was slowing down. Ewan's heart sank. The bull was not stupid enough charge into a wall. It did not want to crack its head open, Ewan's head, however, that would be a different matter.

He could hear the bull trotting, then walking towards him. Was the bull playing with him? Or maybe the bull had lost him because he was standing still? Ewan recalled a natural history documentary claiming that if a rhinoceros charged at you then you should stand still. Rhinos have such bad eyesight they would probably miss anyway. Could the same apply to bulls? Ewan grew up in a city suburb and had no experience of livestock.

He could hear the bull panting, hear it sniffing the ground and the air. Was it trying to sniff him out? *Stay perfectly still*, he told himself.

Ewan was enveloped by the meaty warmth. Then he could see the bull, first the tips of its horns, then the nose ring, then its small eyes and head and finally the boulder of its body came out of the night. Then it stopped completely. Ewan pressed his back against the wall. The bull raised his head and, long and loud, breathed in the night air through its nostrils. There was no way the bull was so blind as to not see Ewan. They were only a metre apart. Ewan could feel the creature's hot breath on his chest, but the bull seemed distracted by something undetectable to Ewan's senses. It swung its head from side to side as if its horns were an aerial picking up a signal. Then the bull began to make little worried whimpers that Ewan would not have thought monstrous bulls ever made. The bull began to back off. Ewan could not believe his luck. It made three or four steps backwards and sank back into the night. Ewan heard it turn around and begin to trot again, back up the field this time, and away.

Ewan collapsed against the wall and listened to it go.

CHAPTER FOURTEEN

Every morning just before dawn Mrs Hooard drove her delivery van up and out of Ballydog and travelled the forty kilometres to the next village. There was a post office there and most mornings she collected the post for Ballydog. Her service was required because the real postmen of County Donegal refused to go anywhere near Ballydog. They were not paid enough to endure those folk they said. Mrs Hooard was the woman to contact if you ever needed anything delivered, she went to the capital and to Derry a couple of times a week as well. Her red van was a common sight on the Ballydog road, a road that otherwise carried very little traffic as the infamously bad town was the only place it went. Mrs Hooard was round and merry-looking. The springy suspension of her van caused her to bounce up and down in her seat wildly as she drove over bumps and potholes. All the while her rosy cheeks glowed and her blue eyes sparkled. She was only rarely tempted to steal any of the interesting packages that passed through her hands. However, on those rare occasions she gave in to the temptation immediately. Her house was full of things that never made it where they were meant to go. Neither could she resist reading all the postcards and throwing away the ones that contained anything too pleasant, such as good news or the word 'sunshine'. She read the postcards while driving back towards town, rolled down her window and tossed out those she could not abide. Throwing away postcards was a great tonic for her, the best part of her day. The postcards would glide away into the bogs along the roadside and she laughed and laughed, bouncing up and down in her seat, her rosy cheeks glowing and her blue eyes sparkling.

In the early morning after Ewan's visit to The Villa, Mrs Hooard was returning to Ballydog. The gearbox was complaining bitterly as she drove up the last rise before the sharp descent into town. She was pressing her substantial weight against the steering wheel in an effort to help her van get over the top. Up ahead a herd of twenty or so cows were trooping down the lane, moving unusually quickly. Their owner, who presumably was behind them, must have been driving them hard, probably with the help of a big stick.

Mrs Hooard swore out loud.

'There is no way I'm stopping on this hill,' she said to herself, 'they'll just have to step aside.'

As they got nearer Mrs Hooard was surprised to see young pigs among the cows, scuttling along between their legs regardless of the danger. A cow's hoof could have brained one of them easily. Then, as the herd and the van passed each other, she saw that things were even stranger.

There was no farmer driving the livestock, they seemed to be going somewhere entirely of their own accord.

And was that Mrs Gin's cat among them?

Mrs Gin would be heartbroken when she found out that her pet cat had run away. This made Mrs Hooard momentarily forget her curiosity about the mismatched herd. Mrs Gin and Mrs Hooard were sisters but one day forty years ago they had a fight over a boy and had not spoken since. Not a single word to each other despite living in the same town, crossing paths at Kilfeather's shop, and attending the same bingo sessions in the town hall. That may sound unlikely but families fractured like that were not unusual in Ballydog. Take the Toil brothers. There were three Toil brothers, aged thirty-five, thirty-eight and forty. None of these brothers had spoken to either of the others in almost eight years, and they all lived in the same house.

Mrs Hooard was overcome with laughter, imagining how her interfering sister, with her permanently shrieking voice, would cry over losing her precious cat. She rocked with great peals of laughter, temporarily lost control of the van and nearly collided with a cow.

What Mrs Hooard saw when she reached the top of the hill made her stop laughing and slam on the brakes. An animal parade was coming up the road. Pigs, goats, dozens of sheep, an old donkey and more cows were all walking together. It looked like all the livestock of Ballydog's farms were involved in the exodus. There were many domestic pets too, cats, dogs and . . . there was Rover, her very own Jack Russell! Mrs Hooard pulled on the handbrake and clambered out of the van, leaving the door open. As Rover approached she put on her sternest look and pointed up into the cab.

'Rover, get in there this second,' she ordered.

Rover ignored her and kept marching.

*   *   *

In the grey light of morning, the farmers gathered in the town square. They left their Land Rovers parked haphazardly around them. None of them had slept a wink. The night before, all their livestock got spooked and refused to settle. They went mad in their fields, stables and pens. Then they started breaking out. Cows backed up to the gates of their fields and kicked them down with their hind legs. Chickens flew from their coops. Most spectacular of all, O'Hara's bull had charged straight through the wall around its field, leaving a bull-shaped hole and a trail of destruction heading east. All the animals were heading east, inland, away from the sea.

The farmers exchanged theories, pointed fingers and crushed cigarette butts under their boots. 'What have we done to deserve this?' they demanded. 'Nothing, nothing at all.' They formed search parties to go and find their animals and drag them back. Not all the animals were leaving by the road, some were crossing the fields or using back lanes. Several farmers brought dogs to help in the hunt. The hounds strained on their leashes and barked. The farmers smiled to see them so energised. But the dogs were not straining on their leashes because they were eager for the hunt. It was because they wanted to escape Ballydog too. The dogs wanted to go inland just like every other animal.

During the day, while the youngsters were at school, more of the animals of Ballydog absconded. One by one or two by two they left Ballydog. Cats and dogs walked side by side. Some owners chased after their pets in their cars. If they caught up with them they threw them in the back seat and attempted to drive home. It was not easy to drive while their cats clawed at them and their dogs pounded themselves against the rear windscreen and howled.

Pet birds escaped and flew east. It was not a good day to clean out a budgie's cage, nor would the next day be.

Unseen animals were also affected. During the night a convoy of badgers had padded silently along the Batter and away from Ballydog. Only the Woman on the Hill, watching from her window, saw them leave. Every mouse of every attic in every house in the estate crept away. Above, bats flitted eastward. The rats that lived in the hotel were checking out. The rats of the Lobster's Cage *wanted to* leave, but they had difficulty motivating themselves. Once, generations ago, this family of rats drank from a puddle of Ponny Dew. Since then they always gnawed a tiny hole in fresh barrels of the concoction. Not a serious leak, just a soft spot in the wood that would gently ooze a supply. They licked at it night and day. Permanently drunk, the rats felt the instinct to escape, an irrepressible urge in most creatures that day, as something more like a hazy suggestion. They put it off until the next day. And the next day they would put it off again . . .

By the time May, Andrew and Ewan finished school, all the animals in Ballydog were gone or going. At least the ones that could were. One that could not was on the edge of town, in the trees beyond the estate, in a glass bowl on a makeshift table, in a place called The Villa. Finn, the goldfish, after spending all night head-butting the inside of its bowl, finally fractured its little skull and floated to the surface, dead.

CHAPTER FIFTEEN

It was getting dark. Andrew kept his hands in his pockets during the walk to the lighthouse. He pulled them out only to remove William's bashed-up watch from his pocket and hurl it into the sea. Ewan did not try to stop him.

'I am sure your drawings mean something,' said Ewan when they were walking again, 'it makes sense to try and find out what.'

Andrew did not reply.

They passed the old pier. Ewan studied the *Sunny Buoy* as they passed. The generator was running and a floodlight attached to the mast lit up the deck but there was no sign of May. Up ahead, over the crest of a hill, the sky began to glow every twelve seconds. The lighthouse had begun its night's work. Crossing the slopes the two boys were soon able to see the tower itself. Its whitewash gleamed in the dark. The whole building seemed to hum softly, it was almost magical. A light was on in the first-floor window, Weir's living quarters. Then the beam of the lighthouse swept around, exposing the boys and their surroundings. It was like a soundless lightning strike. It startled them, then was just as suddenly gone. Twelve seconds later it swung around upon them again. It was almost as disconcerting the third and fourth time. Andrew hated the feeling the light beam gave him, the feeling of being under examination.

'Spooky, isn't it, with the light turning?' said Ewan.

Andrew made a bored sound. 'Shows all you know. The light doesn't turn. What turns is the guard around the light, it's open at one side and closed at the other.'

'I see,' said Ewan. 'That creates the impression of a revolving light.' He was glad to have got Andrew talking, the subject did not matter.

'Do you ever watch *Planet Earth* on Sunday evenings?' asked Ewan. 'I used to never miss it, but now we've no television.'

'I don't watch telly,' said Andrew, 'boring.'

'Oh.'

The beam washed over them a couple more times.

'How come you've got a shaved head?' asked Andrew suddenly. He stopped and looked at Ewan. 'Did you do it so you'd look *hard* when you moved into Ballydog?'

Ewan had thought somebody might say that to him, and he had prepared all sorts of convincing denials. But, when it came to the crunch, his honestly overrode everything.

'Yes,' he conceded as the light passed over them.

'Well, I'll tell you one thing,' said Andrew as he turned away, 'it didn't work.'

The beam had washed over them often by the time they got to the door of the lighthouse. Ewan knocked as solidly as he could. He wanted to be

94

sure Weir would hear them. Andrew kept his hands in his pockets and looked back in the direction of town. They waited for a while, then Ewan knocked again. Weir did not come to the door.

'Perhaps he can't hear us,' said Ewan.

'Why would he want to talk to us?' said Andrew. 'He probably can hear us, he just wants nothing to do with us.'

Ewan feared his unwilling partner was correct about that. He looked up and was almost sure he saw a flash of grey hair disappearing back in the window above them. They waited another couple of minutes and still Mr Weir did not come to the door.

At least this put Andrew in a better humour. 'I didn't want to go in there anyway,' he said. 'I wouldn't trust him, my da says he's half-crazy. Come on, let's go.'

'I suspect if May was with us things would be different,' said Ewan, looking up the tower. He was unwilling to give up. From his pocket he pulled his notebook and pencil and thought about what to say in a note to Weir. Ewan had seen and heard enough strangeness in the last few days to write a whole essay but there was no time for that. With his note he just wanted to make a noise, demand attention. 'What do you know about undiscovered sea creatures?' he wrote. He signed the note, added Andrew's name too, and slipped it under the door.

They went back along the path by the seashore. Andrew was relieved when they had left the area and he no longer had to feel the weight of the lighthouse beam crossing his back.

95

The *Sunny Buoy* was just as they had left it, but now May was standing at the end of the pier. She was looking out over the bay to the waning moon, low on the Atlantic, neatly centred over the mouth of the bay.

'Come with me,' Ewan said. Andrew hung back, but trailed after Ewan in the end. May was easier to handle than Weir would have been. May turned to face them and for a moment, from Ewan's position, the crescent moon in the sky was around her head like a broken halo.

'Hello,' she said. She was surprised to see Ewan, she was surprised to see Andrew, and she was *very* surprised to see the pair of them together.

'Hello,' said Ewan. He felt he should keep his distance; they had her cornered at the end of the pier and he didn't want to scare her.

'May, is anything going on?' Ewan asked. He looked towards the town square of Ballydog where the farmers were gathering again to discuss the problem with their animals. Sound travelled well over the cold water. Angry voices could be heard, their words almost clear enough to be made out. The farmers had lost many animals that day and the livestock they had managed to drag back were trying to break out again. The cows would not be milked and the chickens would not lay.

May stayed quiet, so Ewan went on: 'I have been noticing lots of odd occurrences lately. Do you have any idea what they might mean?'

'Aye, something terrible is goin' to happen,' said May matter-of-factly, 'I don't think it can be stopped. I went to the Woman on the Hill and she agrees. She told me a lot of things actually, I've been thinking about her words ever since . . . I'm

96

not crazy ye know,' she said to Andrew, 'it's a talent.'

Andrew looked at his shoes.

'Are you planning to do anything?' asked Ewan.

'I just wanna get out of here, take the *Sunny Buoy* and me dad and go.'

'Run away?' asked Ewan. He was disappointed.

'Aye. I'm trying to get the engine running again but I can't. It hasn't run in years and I've no notion how to fix it.' She pointed an accusing finger at Andrew. 'I asked him to help me, but he doesn't care.'

Andrew was outnumbered. Events had run out of his control and now he was wrapped up with Weir, Ewan and May. He was on the weirdo side of town, far from The Villa. He hated one thought but could not stop thinking it: maybe this was where he belonged.

'Listen,' said Andrew, 'if it'll keep you happy I'll take a look at the engine. Tomorrow, after school. Now can yous leave me alone?'

Was it the right thing to do? Andrew felt the stomach-flutter that goes with taking a gamble. He had dived into unknown waters. He did not want Ewan and May to know he felt that way. And he certainly did not want his pack to know. Whether doing a thing was right or wrong, good or bad, did not normally concern Andrew. Whether it worked or not was far more important.

Andrew's offer did make May happy and a small smile came loose. Then a loud roar of discontent from the town square brought back her frown. The farmers had been joined by luckless fishermen and factory workers who were in danger of losing their jobs. Fitz was buying-in fish from other towns to keep the factory running but production was much lower than usual. They were all under pressure and angry, but they did not know where to direct their anger.

'Ballydog is in serious trouble,' said May.

'What do you think is going to happen exactly?' asked Ewan.

'I don't know *exactly*,' said May, 'but . . .'

She looked out over the dark water. Every living thing underneath it came to her in an anxious whisper. The fish were long gone but thousands of mussels were still unclamping themselves from the rocks. Soon the whisper would fade to nothing but for now it was like a low, humming choir . . .

Something is coming. Something is coming.
Something big.

CHAPTER SIXTEEN

Big. It was true. The sea creature was the biggest living thing on earth. And, with the exception of some glaciers, it was the largest moving object on the face of the earth. It moved considerably faster than a glacier. After waking and slowly becoming aware of its own size, the creature began to move. Slowly at first; it had not moved in almost a century. Faster as its legs loosened and its anger began to burn. The deep ocean divided to accommodate it, thousands of tonnes of water shifting right and left. Instinct directed the vast creature, it did not know where it was going but it would know when it got there. Then there would be hell to pay.

Why did it do what it did? Could it be stopped?

Nobody has ever offered a satisfactory answer to these questions. The wise men of the Byzantine Empire thought it acted as a kind of surgeon, cutting away parts of the world that had gone bad, before they infected other parts. They said it would live as long as such places exist.

In a similar vein the Native Americans of the north-western seaboard thought of the sea creature as 'the guard dog of the world'. They believed that a cursed place produced an evil pulse, a pulse that could be felt at the bottom of the sea. Eventually it would awaken the sea creature, which would then seek the source of its disturbance.

The creature was too big to be stopped by force. Almost every storyteller, historian and artist agreed on that. However, the Ancient Greeks told a tale in which the sea creature was actually killed. They called it Cetus, and believed it was controlled by Poseidon, the god of the sea. The Greek story about Cetus has been told for centuries. The King and Queen of an African kingdom were going to give their daughter, Andromeda, to the sea creature. She was chained to a rock by the shore and bonfires lit around her. One writer put it like this: 'There burst forth a roar, and waves that made all the land shudder. Lo! Of a sudden there rose from the sea a Beast, of monstrous bulk; not by any mountain, not by the sea we know couldst thou measure it.'

Yet Andromeda was saved. The hero Perseus flew past. He was the son of Zeus and could fly because his sandals had wings. Perseus was returning from slaying the Medusa, a creature with snakes for hair and eyes that turned living things to stone. He was carrying the chopped-off head of the Medusa in his satchel.

Perseus flew down to face the sea creature. He pulled out the Medusa's head and held it before its eyes. The creature was transformed to grey rock and crumbled back into the sea.

According to that myth, Cetus was killed. But it was only a myth. The sea creature that inspired the idea of Cetus was right now charging towards Ballydog. It was not turned to stone. It lived.

The Leveller, Cetus, or the Big Hungry, did not know why it did what it did. Despite its huge size the creature's brain was only the size of a cabbage. It did not think. It did not wonder, *why am I here?* It would not even understand the question. It had only instinct, and anger.

The sea and animal life around Ballydog also had instinct. They knew to get away from the area. They could not have told you why exactly, they just knew they had to. The people of Ballydog felt a similar threat, but human beings have been learning to ignore instinct for thousands of years. They repressed their dark worries. They denied even having them. 'Ignore it and it will go away' could have been Ballydog's motto. Or its epitaph.

CHAPTER SEVENTEEN

The next morning a madness infected Ballydog. A madness that helped the people forget their runaway animals and the fish shortage. *Ravenous Rachel*, a fishing trawler, had returned to port. It had failed to haul a single fish, but it did have something else in its hold. Something exciting.

Rapidly the news spread from person to person. From above Ballydog you could see the news travel. It was like a superbug, an irresistible infection that immediately gripped everybody it touched. As soon as a man, woman or child heard it, they dropped everything and ran down to the new pier. The news entered the Lobster's Cage. All the drunks fell out of the place and headed for the source. It travelled up Main Street, seizing all it found with the need to run to the new pier. Old women at Kilfeather's shop shoved each other out of the way to be first out the door and scurrying down the street. Mothers, gripped by the fever, abandoned their babies in their prams and joined the dash. The priest bolted out of the church and the cashiers leaped over the counter of the bank. The news could not be contained, it was airborne. Up in the estate it travelled from house to house. Within minutes everybody was affected. Front doors were flung open and housewives, still with rubber gloves on their hands and rollers in their hair, tore out and made for the new pier. The youngsters bailed out of the school and the workers burst out of the fish finger factory. Their managers blew their whistles at them but to no avail, so they gave up and ran to the new pier as well. Even Mr Weir left his lighthouse, and the long shiny car parked outside Fitz's house slipped out of the gates and cruised down into town. All to see the *Ravenous Rachel*'s amazing catch.

The catch was hanging from the trawler's crane by chains. It was swung out over the heads of the people standing on the pier. They gaped up at it. The skipper was telling the story of its capture.

The search for fish shoals had brought them many kilometres out to sea, much further than they had ever gone before. They still failed to locate a shoal worth netting. The *Rachel* had been returning to Ballydog with an empty hold and the crew were in dark humour and fighting amongst themselves. It was beginning to look as if one of the crew was going to get picked on and thrown overboard, like a sacrifice to the sea.

Then they saw it: a large dark patch moving slowly a few metres below the surface of the water. The creature was swimming so slowly it was easy to rope. They towed it to port. Nothing could survive being dragged backwards for such a distance. At the pier, when they raised the creature, its huge flippers and ancient head hung heavily. It was dead.

The people of Ballydog let out cheers and shouts. This would be a day to remember.

'That's the biggest turtle I've ever seen or heard of,' said a fisherman.

'It's a leatherback, I bet you.'

'Is it a world record-breaker?' wondered Mr Boyle aloud. 'The biggest ever?'

'If not we could pump a bit of air in it 'til it is,' someone replied.

There were more comments, followed by laughter. The fishermen who had caught and drowned the leatherback were slapped on the back and commended. Fitz parked his car directly on the pier, got out and walked towards the gathered people. You were not allowed to park cars on the pier but nobody was going to say that to him. Without him there would be no new pier at all.

'Good on yous boyos,' said Mrs Hooard to the

crew.

'Maybe we can make fish fingers out of it,' said someone else.

'Maybe so,' said Cody Savage, the captain of the *Rachel*. 'I want to get a few bob for it.'

'I'll buy the shell off you, Cody,' someone called, 'I need a new bathtub.'

When the people saw Fitz they hushed, and parted to let him through. Everyone focused on him. The atmosphere shifted from, *look at the turtle* to *what's Fitz going to say?* Those that loved him and those that hated him too, they all wanted to know what he would say about the catch. He was like a nineteenth-century landlord riding in on his horse, they were the peasants doffing their caps and calling him *squire*. He was like the United States, they were the small Latin American countries whose economies depended on it. He was like the Tyrannosaurus Rex, they were a herd of tree-munching vegetarians worrying about their nests.

Fitz walked in a circle, gazing up at the prize. 'Well, well, well, what have we here?' he was heard to utter. Some folk began to answer but then realised it was a rhetorical question. There was very little that Fitz didn't know.

Fitz extended his arms and said loudly, 'I won't be surprised if that is the largest leatherback ever caught here or anywhere else.'

The roar of approval that burst from the crowd was like an oil strike. The cheering went on for at least two minutes. Fitz folded his arms and enjoyed it. Above him the corpse of the Old Man of the Sea revolved in the breeze, water dripping off his flippers and running off the channels of his shell.

'Speech,' somebody called to him from the crowd.

'Oh yes, speech,' shrieked Mrs Gin.

Fitz was still smiling and said, 'Yes, it is a good day for a speech.'

On his word people sprang to work. Men stacked a few pallets on top of each other as a stage. Someone fetched a microphone and an amplifier before remembering there was nowhere to plug it in. Strings of festival flags were found and hung from the turtle. Children were sent up to the town hall to bring chairs so the old folks wouldn't strain their poor knees. The people of Ballydog loved speeches and it was well known that Fitz gave the best. They could hardly wait.

Less than ten minutes later, Fitz stepped up on the stage provided for him. He gave the turtle another glance and announced, 'I reckon we might have a record breaker here!' There was a short cheer before he went on, 'And it's the most unusual catch that has ever been hauled into Ballydog. Congratulations to the crew of the *Rachel*. You've done a fine job.' There was a round of applause.

'But let's not just leave it at that. I see big potential here and if we use our brains we can make something of it. The question is, what are we going to do with this fine specimen? Well, I reckon I have the answer.'

The crowd were delighted. None of them had any answers. Up until a moment before they had not even realised there was a question.

'I reckon this could be a new beginning for our town. Let me explain myself, ladies and gentlemen.

For years now we have watched every other town up and down this coast making a fortune every summer. Off the back of what? TOURISM! That's what. What have those towns got that we haven't?'

The truth was quite a lot. Ballydog was the ugliest, meanest and most bitter town in Ireland. And, although they would never admit it, the people of Ballydog knew this was why nobody visited.

'Attractions!' shouted Fitz, pointing up at the leatherback. '*That's* what they have and now, if we play our cards right, Ballydog will have one as well. We all know of a certain town in County Kerry with a dolphin swimming about in the harbour. It swam in one day years ago and has been living there ever since. The town pet it is. Tourists pour into the place to get a look. While visiting they fill up the hotels, eat five-course meals, and toss money around in the street. That dolphin is worth six million a year to the town.'

The air was charged with excitement at the mention of such a big number.

One fisherman saw a problem with what Fitz was saying and although contradicting Fitz was not done often he could not help but stammer, 'But Mr Fitzpatrick, this is nothing like that dolphin, this turtle is dead.'

'Exactly,' said Fitz, 'even better, it won't swim away on us, will it? I'll get a taxidermist over from the city, we'll get the thing stuffed. Put it in a glass case. Charge admission to look at it. Ten euro for adults, five for children . . .'

'Ten euro whatever age you are,' called Heiferon from his place in the crowd. There was an enormous cheer. Hearts raced.

105

'We could build an interpretive centre, we'll have bus-loads of tourists arriving. French, Germans, Yanks!'

'Wonderful! Wonderful!' Mrs Gin shrieked.

'You could start a bed and breakfast, Mrs Gin,' said Fitz. He laughed and gave her a wink. She went red and shrieked, 'I'd be good at that!'

Fitz went on, 'I propose we use the town hall to display it. I'll ring a taxidermist this very day. I'll tell him he'll need every bit of stuffing he can get his hands on!'

There was laughter and cheering. Fitz was amazing. He thought of all the brilliant answers to all the brilliant questions that he had thought of as well.

But there were murmurs of protest. The older ladies were objecting to losing the town hall to the turtle. Where would they play their bingo on a Monday, Tuesday, Wednesday, Thursday, Friday and Saturday evening? And sometimes a Sunday afternoon as well? They liked bingo.

'Shut up, you and your bingo,' men shouted at them, 'the town needs the money.' The women shouted back insults.

'The bingo is the only bit of pleasure I get,' shrieked Mrs Gin.

Fitz was shaking his head but smiling as well. It was a lucky thing he was there to watch over them. He raised his hands and gradually the crowd quietened.

'Ladies and gentlemen, I see a simple solution. You need a big room to play your bingo? Use the church. It's empty all evening.'

Brilliant. The crowd went wild. They all agreed the church would be a lovely place to play bingo.

106

The number caller could stand in the pulpit. But then Father Fingers, suppressing his terror, staggered out of the crowd and stood in front of Fitz's stage. His hands were shaking. 'I am sorry, sir,' he was heard to stammer by the people standing closest to him. 'I am afraid that I cannot allow the church to be used for bingo. It just would not be *proper*. The bishop might hear about it and then . . . then . . .' His head fell at the thought of possible consequences.

Fitz stood looking down at him. He had expected Finger's objection before he even suggested using the church. He had expected objections to using the town hall as well.

The crowd muttered and complained under their breaths. Some booed the priest out loud, but it was clear they had to indulge him. The church was his place, unfortunately. Then the mob became uneasy; would they lose their tourism industry before it had even begun?

Only one man could save them.

Fitz started pacing back and forth across the stage. He was thinking.

'Okay, a new idea,' said Fitz. 'The town hall is too small anyway for the crowds arriving next summer. We have only one building in this town big enough to display our treasure, but it will mean great financial risk for me.'

The crowd hushed.

'But still, it would be good for the town,' he was saying to himself, 'we could all stand to gain.'

He stopped and faced the people. 'Maybe, just maybe, we could use my factory.' A wave of excitement passed through the crowd.

'Yes, please, Mr Fitzpatrick, it would be

perfect,' said Heiferon. There were murmurs of agreement. The people began to discuss the merits of the idea among themselves. There was no fish anyway, might as well use the building for something else.

Then Fitz burst their bubble. 'No, I'm sorry,' he said and turned away. 'Right now the factory is not making money because we have no fish, but the fish stocks are bound to go back to normal soon. I would have to be a fool to convert the building just because of a few bad days.'

'Please, Mr Fitzpatrick,' someone cried.

'We need the factory!' said another.

Fitz gave the crowd a long, solemn look. Some said later that there had been fatherly love in that look. Breaths were held. Fitz was thinking hard. The crowd watched him desperately.

'I will help you, we can convert the factory but on one condition. If you agree there will be no rent to pay and I will take care of everything: the preparations, the advertising, the taxidermy and the display. With a major attraction in town we will all gain. It will be a golden era for Ballydog, but I built that factory and I own everything in it and if the animal is to be displayed in it then I will have to own it too. Give me the turtle and I will give you a tourist attraction.'

Captain Savage was immediately hounded to answer Fitz. There was no need to discuss it. He swelled with pride and confirmed he was delighted to hand over today's catch to Mr Fitzpatrick. The people celebrated. Hands were shaken. Photographs were taken. The deal was done.

A celebration took place under the dead turtle for an hour after Fitz's speech. The people of

Ballydog were able to forget their worries for a while; the loss of all the animals and the disappearance of all the fish. They also were able to forget the pressure that was building up between their ears, the pressure that felt like an instinct and got stronger every day. Nobody talked about it. It was easy to avoid the subject now they had something to distract them. Rich tourists would be arriving soon. They could almost see the tour buses coming over the top of the hill already. While celebrating and admiring the turtle, the people began dreaming up money-grabbing schemes. Now that Ballydog was set to be a tourist destination each of them wanted a piece of the action. They cheered and clapped and at the same time plotted and eyed their neighbours suspiciously. Schemes were already taking shape and new jealousies forming among them.

None of this mattered, of course. They were all doomed.

CHAPTER EIGHTEEN

Not quite all the people of Ballydog were there to see the turtle and hear Fitz's grand plan. The Woman on the Hill remained in her cottage, on her hill. She was unaware of the excitement in the town centre but would not have been interested anyway. May did not go to the pier either, although she did know what had happened. She could see the huge corpse of the Old Man of the Sea, hung in the air, from the deck of the *Sunny Buoy*. She saw the townsfolk celebrating and heard

109

their cheers. She pressed herself into a corner of the wheelhouse and clasped her hands over her ears. May's teeth clamped together like a vice. Her whole body curled and became as tight as a knot. She would be hard to unpick.

It was getting dark by the time May finally pulled herself out of the corner. She was aching all over. Gingerly she extended her sore arms and legs, as if she was afraid they might have turned to glass. Eventually she was recovered enough to go out onto the deck and start the generator. Then she switched on the mast-light and ran the pump for five minutes. Andrew was coming, if he kept his promise. May would not tell Andrew about her friendship with the ancient leatherback, she would not tell anyone. She would just have to forget about him. It was just another bad day in Ballydog.

When he arrived Andrew wanted to get straight down to business. He threw open the engine covering and examined the engine. May fetched him the torch she kept in the wheelhouse, hooked behind the wheel.

'Diesel,' he said. 'I thought it would be, you can tell because there aren't any spark plugs.'

May was relieved to hear that he knew what he was talking about. Or at least he seemed to.

'Have ye ever worked on a boat engine before?' May asked him timidly.

'You don't even know what you have got here. No, I have not worked on many boat engines but I *have* worked on tractor engines and this is a tractor engine, converted for use in a boat.'

The *Sunny Buoy* was not a complicated boat; a starter switch, a wheel, a prop, a rudder, a tractor engine, a throttle, a pump and some lights were all

110

it had.

Andrew lowered himself down into the bilge alongside the engine. 'It's badly corroded but it looks like it should still run. There doesn't seem to be anything missing. Go into the wheelhouse and try starting her up.'

Andrew pulled out the dipstick and sighed at the result. May did as she was told. She turned the starter switch several times. Nothing happened. Not the gasping sound of a failed start-up, not the shudder of pistons, nothing.

'Could be the starter motor,' said Andrew, 'you've a hand-wheel here, I'll try starting it by hand.'

'I've already tried that,' said May, back on deck and looking down at him. 'Couldn't get it to turn, not even a wee bit.'

'Yeah, well, you're a girl,' said Andrew. He placed his hands over the rusty handle of the starter wheel. With all his might he attempted to turn it. It did not even move a millimetre.

'Corrosion,' said Andrew, 'rusted tight.'

'Aye, that must be it,' said May.

'Still looks like it should run, though,' said Andrew, 'it's pretty dry down here.'

'I keep the bilge pumped out,' said May.

Andrew waved his hand over the engine dismissively. 'I can get this thing working no bother, but it will take a bit of time. It's just rusted up and needs a cleaning. The parts are seized, you're out of oil, there's only a drop of diesel in the tank and the air filter is all rotted. And you keep filling up with water because the seal around the propeller shaft is rotted too, but that isn't a big problem if you don't want to go very far.' He

111

looked up at her and asked, 'You don't want to go very far, do you?'

May realised that Andrew was curious about her plan. He was starting to feel the danger too. What would it take for him to admit it? That was not so important. May now knew that Andrew was going to get the *Sunny Buoy* running, even if he had to come back every night for a week.

Ewan arrived. Andrew sank back down to continue examining the engine, muttering something about the 'Northboy'.

'I think the lighthouse keeper knows something about the Big-Boss,' said Ewan. He was standing at the railing of the *Sunny Buoy* looking towards the glow from the lighthouse. May was standing beside him.

'Aye, maybe so. Andrew knows more than he lets on too,' she said. 'To be honest I don't care who knows what. I just wanna be able to get out of its way.'

Andrew grunted and complained as he pulled off the fan belt's covering.

'It will arrive from the sea,' said Ewan.

'Then I better get a head start on it. That's the way I plan on leaving.'

'Aren't you curious to know more about it? Perhaps we don't have to run.'

'There's no shame in running from a place like Ballydog,' said May.

*　　　*　　　*

At school the next day Andrew's pack wanted to know why he had not shown up at The Villa.

'Helping my da strip an old engine in our

112

garage,' he said. 'He's making me help him but I don't really mind.'

Sure enough, his hands were the colour of rust. Mushroom's eyes narrowed, he had seen hands in a very similar condition just lately. A girl's hands.

'It's a big job so we might be a few more nights yet,' said Andrew.

In class, Andrew still barely spoke to Ewan. Ewan was sorely tempted to say something to him but he could see Andrew was a boy sitting on a fence. It would be risky to tip him. There was no way to tell on which side he would fall.

In class Heiferon ran a competition. The object was to come up with a slogan for Ballydog. He claimed the town needed one now it was set to become a major tourist destination. Heiferon said he would push for the slogan to be used on a billboard advertising campaign, a campaign that he was going to propose to Mr Fitzpatrick himself. Millions of people would see the advert and read the winning slogan. He wanted it punchy and persuasive. In the end Niccy Lynch came third with, 'Ballydog: like it, or else!' Job Flattery came second with, 'Visit Ballydog, you'll never get over it', but it was Mushroom who won the competition with, 'Ballydog: Bad is the new Good'.

*   *   *

'I'm getting there,' said Andrew that night after a few hours' work. 'We'll need to buy a drum of diesel and a couple of other bits and pieces so I hope you have something in your piggy bank.'

May had nothing but Ewan said, 'I have some money, don't worry about it.'

113

'Grand,' said Andrew. 'Next you'll clean and oil each part and I'll put it back together. It is not broken, just seized up. It'll take a couple more nights but I'll do it for you, just don't tell anybody else. If you do, I won't be back . . . hey!'

Ewan and May had stopped listening. They were watching a thin line of pinkish light cutting through the sky over the mouth of the bay.

'What's that?' said Andrew.

'A small jet plane, perhaps?' said Ewan.

It was coming directly towards Ballydog, but very low and Ballydog had no airstrip.

As the jet-propelled object zoomed closer, the youngsters saw it was not a plane but a man, strapped to some kind of flying machine. The man saw them too. He let go of the controls for a moment and waved at them. That was a mistake. His craft veered out of control and it took a few dangerous seconds for him to stabilise again. Then he obviously decided that the old pier was a good landing place for him. He lined himself up with the pier and cut the engine. The blast of red energy pumping out of the base of the jetpack vanished, leaving the man to glide in the rest of the way on its small wings. His feet hit the end of the pier and he dug in his heels, the metallic soles of his boots streaming sparks as he came to a grinding halt on the pier in front of the three youngsters.

May and the boys were struck dumb by this dramatic arrival. The man was quite calm; he stood there and looked about, checking out the bay and the countryside. Then his nostrils twitched. The burning smell from the flying machine had dissipated and he had just caught the fishy smell of Ballydog for the first time. The

114

man's uniform was like a soldier's, although without insignia. It was all black, made of leather, canvas and dark steel, and had many pockets, buckles, zips and holsters containing clunky instruments and tools. He was not a big man, but his uniform and the machine on his back made him look huge. The flying machine was higher than his head, it completely overwhelmed his body. An arm, loaded with guide-stick and buttons, jutted out of it. This was how he controlled his flights and landings. The man had a smug look on his face. He had always loved the reaction his arrivals received. He savoured May, Ewan and Andrew's awed expressions.

'My name is Alexander Bam Brilski Teodors,' he said in a slightly high-pitched and Russian-sounding accent. 'Also known as the Hunter. I have a few other names as well, but those are enough to begin with.'

'A hunter of what?' asked Andrew.

'*The* Hunter. What do I hunt? You have not heard of me. This is because I work covertly. The people who contract me want everything hush-hush. I operate in the shadows. Ya, the *shadows*.' He liked his new phrase. 'They have their reasons. I *could* tell you about the contract I have just did for a Brazilian corporation but then . . .' he leaned forward and whispered, 'they might find out and kill you.'

With the weight of the jetpack he barely managed to straighten himself up again. 'So, I will not tell you. What I *will* tell you is this. I hunt dangerous creatures. Real living monsters. What do you think of that?'

'Yes,' Ewan confirmed to the others, 'I emailed

him. I didn't expect to even get a reply let alone have him show up like this.'

'Ya, I happened to be passing,' said Alexander Bam Brilski Teodors, also known as the Hunter. 'I was being flown back to Latvia after completion of my last contract. They loaned me a jet and pilot. I made a good job for them. Crossing the north Atlantic I remembered your contact so I got the coordinates of your village. I told the pilot go down to lower altitude and I hopped off. This is good fortune to fly in and find you so fast. You are younger than I expected but I save anyone.'

'Is that thing really fuelled by "the plasma of a fire-breathing salamander"?' asked Ewan.

'My jetpack?' asked the Hunter, patting the controls affectionately. 'Ya, sure is.'

'Are there really such things as fire-breathing salamanders?'

'Not any more,' said the Hunter. 'Fire-breathing salamanders are extinct for three hundred years. Hunted out of existence by men like me.' The Hunter thumped his chest before going on: 'Let's say a certain battalion, stationed in, say as example, Siberia, found the body of a twenty-foot salamander preserved in the ice. Maybe I was there, maybe not. The creature was long-dead of course, but scientists were able to get full DNA chains from it. With them, in laboratories, they were able to recreate its plasma. Is great for propulsion, more efficient than jet fuel.' He patted the controls again. 'But enough of that, you say there is an unlisted creature coming this way. Is it here yet?'

'No, not yet,' Ewan told him, 'and we three are the only people who know about it.'

116

Andrew shuffled awkwardly, he didn't know anything. He was just helping May because he felt sorry for her. May, for her part, watched the stranger with a barely concealed mistrust.

'Ya?' said Teodors. 'Let us perform a test then, boys and girl, call it research.'

He pulled his arms back so as to slip out of the straps of the jetpack but, like a little boy with too many books in his school bag, he began to totter and almost fell over. Eventually he managed to shake it loose and the heavy apparatus hit the pier with a loud *clunk*. The man looked small and weak without it, at least in comparison with the grand opinion he had of himself. At the back and sides of the pack were storage pockets. He unzipped the smallest. It was lined with plastic to keep the contents dry, a few dozen small seeds.

'This is the Dimwheat seed. It comes from my country. It reacts to the aggressive energies and instincts of monsters. If there is one nearby it begins to grow. The bigger the plant, the closer the creature. Simple.' He held up one of the seeds between his thumb and forefinger. 'It is an indicator.'

May, Ewan and Andrew stepped onto the pier to better see what he was doing. Teodors did not plant the seed. He just knelt down and placed it on the flat surface of one of the stones making up the pier. He watered it by spitting on it. Immediately a green shoot burst from seed. It grew a centimetre along the ground before turning upwards into the air. Then it paused.

The Hunter stepped back and sharply looked around. He brought his hand up to his belt and the youngsters were alarmed to see that he was armed with a pistol. He undid the buckle that held it in place but did not withdraw it. What was he seeing or hearing? To May, Ewan and Andrew, it was clear that the Hunter himself was the most dangerous thing in Ballydog that night. It was the speed of the Dimwheat's growth that seemed to have put him on edge. He turned back around to face the youngsters.

'This is interesting result,' he said. 'If we were crossing Siberian ice-lake now there would be a man-eating Chill Fish right beneath our feet, but we aren't. If we were in the Amazon we would already have a giant cobra wrapped around us, squeezing us to death, but we aren't. There is no immediate threat at all. So why does the Dimwheat react so strong?'

They looked down at the newborn plant. It had grown another half-centimetre. The Hunter looked up at the teenagers sharply, as if he suddenly suspected they were hiding something.

'Tell me, how *big* is this thing of yours?' he said.

Ewan looked at May, thinking that she might have some idea. She did not, but judging by the expression on her face she would not have told Teodors if she did. The Hunter seemed oblivious to her mistrust. Meanwhile Andrew was watching the plant, his eyes widening. There was silence as the green shoot made another tiny stretch for the sky.

'It's . . .' Andrew stammered, 'it's gotta be the biggest living thing in the ocean. It won't even all fit in Ballydog Bay. Half of it will have to stay out at sea. Six or seven miles long, it could swallow a fishing boat whole.'

'How are you knowing this, boy?' the Hunter

inquired with one eyebrow raised.

Andrew hung his head. 'I see it in dreams.'

'Ya-ya, premonitions.' The Hunter folded his arms, satisfied. 'I have heard of such things, and the plant agrees with you. It is hard to be sure, but if it is that size, and the Dimwheat continues to grow at that rate, then it looks like you have about a week. Maybe less. I did not know monsters so big existed. It would be expensive to stop a monster of that size.' He wrinkled his nose in the direction of the town square. 'I doubt your town could afford it. Still, I will figure out the charge. Call it research.'

He began to add up figures, talking to himself in his own language and listing things with the aid of his fingers.

'I just want him to go,' May said quietly to Ewan and Andrew.

Andrew shrugged, he was pale and exhausted-looking.

'Let's see what we can learn from him,' reasoned Ewan.

'The job would cost in region of seven millions of your euros,' announced the Hunter.

This was an inconceivable figure to the youngsters. All the people of Ballydog put together, even including Fitz, did not have that much money.

'Can you not help us for the sake of it?' Andrew asked. 'Ballydog doesn't have that kind of money.'

'Despatching monsters is my work, it is true,' said the Hunter. 'But I do not work for free.'

'Why would it be so expensive, Mr Hunter?' asked Ewan.

'There is a set of standard costs, it is dangerous

and skilled work. The salamander's plasma, for example, is highly expensive. But most of the price goes on just one item and getting it here. A nuclear warhead is hard to get and transport, but I have the connections.'

'Nuclear warhead!' they cried in unison.

'Just one!' he protested, 'and I can intercept the monster way off the coast.'

'I really don't think you should set off nuclear devices in the ocean, Mr Hunter,' said Ewan evenly.

'It would cause a fuss, it is true,' he admitted.

Then May stepped forward. She had had enough.

'Listen to me now, ye eejit,' she said, 'we don't want your help, we don't even want ye here in Ballydog, just leave. Go on. Go back to your own country.'

She pointed back out to sea.

Ewan and Andrew were surprised by her outburst but they did not argue with her.

Teodors was taken aback. He shook his head, then laughed at May.

'This often happens, little girl,' he said. 'People contact me because they are afraid. *Please stop the monster, kind sir*. And I say *ya, I will save you*, but when I tell them what I will do to save them they are disgusted: *go away go away, you very bad man*. But what do you expect? To fight a monster you often must be a monster yourself. That is life.'

'Scram, will ye!' said May through gritted teeth.

The Hunter scooped up the Dimwheat and dropped it in one of his many pockets. Then he crouched down and slipped his arms back into the straps of the jetpack. 'You have wasted my time,' he said angrily as he struggled to stand up. 'I could have gone straight home in a corporate jet, instead I am in this stinking town.'

He grabbed at the controls of the jetpack. The salamander's plasma roared into action, producing heat, noise, and lift. True, the blast of the jetpack did look and smell like the breath of a mythical creature. The youngsters covered their eyes and backed off quickly, but not quickly enough to stop their hair getting singed. As the Hunter rose from the pier he shouted, 'A dangerous monster comes this way; be smart, leave town.'

He did a spin in the air and tore off, leaving a fiery-pink streak across the black sky.

'You shouldn't have chased him off,' Andrew snapped at May. 'He could've helped us.'

'He did help us,' said Ewan, 'his plant confirmed Ballydog is in danger and that we have a few days to work with. And I think he helped us in a more important way.'

'Such as?' said Andrew.

'We were finally able to make you admit to knowing about it.'

Andrew huffed.

'I don't *know* anything. I've had nightmares, that's all.'

'Premonitions, perhaps?'

Andrew sank his hands in his pockets.

'Yeah, maybe.'

May was looking at the fading mark that the Hunter had left in the sky. She decided to explain why she had wanted rid of him so badly.

'The Woman on the Hill told me we'd be betrayed by a man coming *down to us from on high*,' she said. 'That was the first thing I thought of when he arrived, flying out of the sky like that. It was him she predicted, I'm sure.'

May looked at the boys. She had calmed down.

'I hope we don't see him again,' she said. 'That would be bad.'

So they would see him again, of course.

CHAPTER NINETEEN

Dawn, and across Ballydog lights were coming on unusually early in the windows of many houses. People were being woken by bad dreams. Unable to return to sleep they went downstairs to their kitchens. They looked out of their windows, towards the sea, as their kettles boiled.

There were other strange occurrences. Some of the students at Ballydog Secondary claimed to have seen a UFO the previous night. They said a bright light had been zipping about over the old pier.

'Nonsense, there is some logical explanation,' said Heiferon gruffly, although with a hint of unease. He had been troubled by bad dreams the night before. 'May! Did you see or hear anything *quare* at the old pier last night?'

'No,' said May and she turned back to the window.

'God help you, girl,' said Heiferon. 'You see and hear odd things every day of the year apart from the one time something actually happened.'

*   *   *

During breaks May and Ewan had taken to sitting under the leafless tree together, an arrangement that caused plenty of amusement among the rest of the class. They did not care.

'The town feels quieter than usual,' said Ewan as he rubbed his head. He was letting his hair grow back and it felt pleasant under his fingertips.

'Aye, that's 'cos the seagulls are leaving,' said May.

Andrew was leading his pack to their place at the back of the boiler house. He acted like he did not see Ewan and May. Mushroom paused and looked at them under the tree. A few of the pack, a splinter group, stopped with him. Mushroom was in the middle of composing a comment when Andrew spoke, 'Leave them alone.' He had not stopped walking. He had not even looked over his shoulder. Andrew was taking a risk. He thought for a moment about how doing right was often riskier than doing wrong.

I'll look out for them this time, he thought to himself, *but they better not get used to it.*

Mushroom was about to object, but all the boys had already trailed after Andrew.

'You're right about the seagulls,' Ewan said to May after the pack had gone.

Ballydog's seagulls had hung on longer than any other bird, but now their numbers were decreasing. In Ewan's first days in town there were hundreds of them, constantly circling or standing in lines along rooftops. Their screeching and squawking had filled the air. Now the sky was almost empty. He looked up at the roof of the school. There were only five or six seagulls there. It should have been dozens.

'What do ye hear when ye listen to gulls?' May asked him.

He listened to their unpleasant screams for a few moments.

'A *terr, terr, terr* noise, over and over again,' he said.

'Aye, gulls are always repeating themselves. But I hear something different.'

May looked up at the seagulls and squinted her eyes. She concentrated hard. Ewan was witnessing something not many people had seen. At least not with an understanding of what was actually happening. May was tuning into things beyond his understanding. For a few seconds that place, under the leafless tree, in a concreted yard, in a town called Ballydog, felt like the very centre of the universe.

'Terror is coming, terror is coming, terror is—'

She broke off and took a breath.

'That is what I hear,' she said.

Just then the seagulls launched upwards and flew east.

'Ye know it's just as well all the birds and animals are leaving Ballydog,' said May, 'I don't wanna be distracted by them for a while.'

*　　　*　　　*

But most of the people of Ballydog *did* want to be distracted.

And now, at last, they had something to distract them. Fitz was to have an unveiling celebration in the fish finger factory when the preservation of the turtle was complete. The leatherback was currently stored in the refrigeration unit of the factory, awaiting the taxidermist. The job would not take long and the unveiling would take place some evening within the week. Everyone was invited, it would be a big night. The party was the talk of the town.

'Fitz is sure to arrange a fine do,' Mr Kilfeather said to all his customers.

'He's ordered an extra-large barrel of Ponny Dew from me specially,' said Conn McKann, leaning against Kilfeather's counter. 'The drink will be flowing!'

'And there'll be sausage rolls, probably,' said Patsy Leary.

'I love sausage rolls,' shrieked Mrs Gin, 'don't you?'

'I am a vegetarian,' said Miss Cancer.

*   *   *

In the evening a van paused at the crest of the hill so the driver could take in the view of the town, bay and the horizon beyond. The letters on the side of the van spelled: 'J J Fuller, Taxidermist'. He released the handbrake and the van slid into the town square and parked outside the factory. Fitz himself was there to meet the taxidermist. He brought him inside to where the catch was lying on three steel tables pushed together. The turtle's flippers had gone rigid and his shell was beginning to wrinkle. He had just been pulled out of the refrigeration unit and was covered in a thin coat of frost. Fuller was wearing a white coat and carrying a wooden toolbox, hacksaw blades protruding from it. He looked like a cross between a surgeon and a washing-machine repair man.

Fuller was astounded by the size of the turtle. He walked around it several times, taking it in. Then, and very quickly, he seemed to fall in love with the corpse. He sniffed at the shell and stroked the flippers.

'I'll need to get it turned over. I'll make my incisions across the underbelly.'

'Sure,' said Fitz. 'I'll use a forklift to flip it.'

'There will be a lot of surplus material from a specimen so large,' said Fuller.

'Any waste can be thrown in the sea,' said Fitz, 'or left out for the seagulls.'

'Oh no,' said Fuller. He looked at his employer with a gleam. 'Have you ever tried turtle stew?'

*   *   *

From the other side of the square May had watched Fitz and the taxidermist shake hands and go inside. She knew what was going on. Soon the taxidermist would get to work on the leatherback. Slice him open, empty out his true flesh and blood and refill him with junk. He would preserve the Old Man of the Sea right at the edge of life, and deny him proper death. The leatherback would be caught, permanently chilled. A mockery of himself.

May closed her eyes and suddenly, with a white flash, she learned the meaning of the word 'hate'. Her face contorted. She hated Ballydog completely, every puddle, pebble and every single person. It was so blinding and powerful she feared that her head might explode with it. Hate was not black, she discovered, nor red, but the purest brightest white. It burned. After a few moments the intensity passed, her face and body

126

unclenched. May had experienced pure hate, a barrier had been broken. Things might never be the same again.

I've got to get out of this place, she thought.

The two people she needed to help her do that very thing were walking towards her across the square. Darkness was descending and Andrew and Ewan were ready for work. They stopped side by side before her and looked at her expectantly, not saying anything. They knew something was wrong. May just turned around and headed for the *Sunny Buoy*, the boys following behind.

CHAPTER TWENTY

The glow from the lighthouse began rising and falling in the sky beyond the slopes.

Andrew squeezed down by the engine and methodically removed and replaced its parts. Up on deck, Ewan and May greased them and handed them back. Andrew had a worry. One of the cogs was so corroded that Andrew thought it would not turn the shaft. Its teeth would disintegrate as soon as the engine began driving it. *Sunny Buoy* wouldn't get very far then. The part would have to be replaced, but where could he get a replacement? Then he heard a voice.

'Playing house, are we?'

Andrew sank down further into the bilge. He knew the voice immediately. It was the unmistakable sneer of Mushroom. He heard Mushroom step onto the deck, followed by the heavy footfall of Tonne.

127

Up on deck, Ewan turned to face them.

It was not just Mushroom and MacPherson. Most of the pack were standing on the old pier. May and Ewan were so wrapped up in their work they had not seen them until they were alongside the *Sunny Buoy*. It had been Mushroom's idea to go there and look for Andrew. If they caught Andrew there with the Northboy and the weirdo girl then he would be a terrible traitor. Andrew would no longer be boss, of course, but that would be the least of his worries. Mushroom had a streak of viciousness it would normally take forty years to develop. And Tonne MacPherson would do anything he was told.

The rest of the pack hesitated on the pier. The *Sunny Buoy* was the home of May and her father. They would not go so far as to step onto it. Mushroom was different. He made towards the exposed engine, there was plenty of room down there for Andrew to be hiding in. Lightly Ewan stepped into his way. Mushroom snorted.

'Tonne, get over here,' he said.

Tonne had just kicked over an upside-down bucket as if he thought Andrew might be hiding under it. It was possible he really did think that. It was hard to tell with Tonne MacPherson. At Mushroom's command he moved towards Ewan.

Need plan . . . thought Ewan. *Plan.*
Plan.

He could not think of one.

Then there was a new voice.

'Why don't you boys go on home to your mammies? I am here to see the woman of the house.'

Everyone looked towards this dominating voice.

128

It was Mr Weir, the lighthouse keeper, walking briskly down the pier.

'Nothing much going on here,' Mushroom said. He turned away from Ewan and put on an innocent face. MacPherson grunted as he slowly registered that the balance of power had shifted.

'Well, go do nothing elsewhere,' said Weir. '*Adios.*'

Mushroom threw a look around him that said: *you were lucky this time.* He stepped back onto the pier and MacPherson clambered after him. Weir watched as the gang sloped away. When they were far enough away to satisfy him, Weir smiled at May and asked brightly, 'Permission to come aboard, my dear?'

She nodded and Weir stepped on. 'I am glad to see your northern friend is here too. I got your note, son. Brief and to the point, I like that. Ah ha . . . *and* the other one. Wonderful.'

Andrew had just poked his head up.

Weir leaned against the railing, rubbed his hands together and said, 'So, let's talk about a certain beast.'

May told Weir what the Woman on the Hill had told her. Weir was interested but not surprised. Ewan told him about the Hunter, the Dimwheat and the reports he had seen on the news and the internet. He also told him about Andrew's drawing and how it had been an exact match for Weir's own. Andrew stayed in the bilge, only his head emerged and he nodded it or shook it at the appropriate times.

'I have done other charcoals like it,' said Weir. 'But it is hardly *me* who does them at all. I don't remember drawing them half the time.' He

129

laughed.

Andrew was amazed Weir could be so relaxed about the trances. To Andrew producing those pictures felt like losing his mind. He had done others as well, drawings that nobody knew about. He always tore them up or burned them.

'Have you been having dreams about it too?' Weir asked Andrew.

'Over a week now,' he replied. 'It's getting to the stage that I can hardly sleep.'

'I have been having those dreams for two months,' said Weir.

Andrew shivered at the thought.

Weir went on, 'I believe other people in Ballydog are having similar nightmares by now. It's no surprise. I consider it only natural. When a life form as big and destructive as that beast is bearing down on a place it can be sensed there. It can be felt in our hearts. Animals are most sensitive to their instincts, we saw their reaction. A sixth sense has started humming, it is trying to get us to pay attention to it. I believe only the most sensitive and brave people will ever look closely enough at these feelings to understand them. Ballydog lacks those kind of people, which is why the situation has become so bad. I am glad to finally meet one.'

Weir smiled at Andrew but Andrew looked away. He knew that he did not deserve that praise. It was the Northboy who had made him face facts.

'Another thing we are short of in Ballydog is people who are not afraid to speak out. The fools,' Weir gestured over the water towards the town centre, 'they would do anything rather than have people think they were strange. They would rather live in quiet desperation. When the beast arrives,

130

they'll die that way.'

'We're goin' to leave,' said May. 'I wanna get me and me dad and our home away from here before it arrives. That's why we're fixing up the engine. We're just goin' to go out the bay and down the coast a wee bit. As far as the next town will do us. Anybody else who wants to can escape with us. You'd be welcome yourself. Maybe ye could help me explain the situation to me dad? He won't listen to me.'

'I could,' Weir said, looking to where the horizon had disappeared between the equally dark sky and sea. 'But first, I would like you to listen to *my* plan. It's very different from yours but with your help, and with the *Sunny Buoy* here, it might just work. It means *not* running away . . . it means facing the beast. I believe we can save the town.'

The youngsters looked at each other.

'Tell us,' said Ewan.

'I delayed coming here and speaking to you,' said Weir, 'because I was not sure if it was right to ask for your help. It is not a completely safe plan. There will be danger.'

Andrew pulled himself up from the bilge and sat on the deck.

'There's a lot of information about the beast still to be found,' Weir began. 'Hardly anybody believes in it any more but it is described in myths and legends. I found physical descriptions of it and stories about what drives it. You know it intends to destroy Ballydog, don't you? But do you know why? Simple. Because it's bad, that's why. Like the way Sodom incurred the wrath of God. But I believe we can stop this cycle of badness. Those dreams and trances were signs. Be strong now and

131

do the right thing and we can counteract the evil of years. I don't claim to have any great love for Ballydog myself but I have taken the role of keeping the bay safe as my work and I don't want to stop now. You can help me. I believe we've been chosen.'

Ewan's heart did a double beat. Andrew gulped.

'Let me tell you all a story,' said Weir, 'this is a true story. Well, it's a legend but based on real events.

'There were three clans along Scotland's east coast locked in permanent war with each other. No one could remember what had started it. The blacksmiths had forgotten how to make ploughs, so long had they been making swords. Running such a long and complicated war meant frequent meetings of the three clans' elders. They would pick some neutral spot and all gather together, often in their dozens, to decide where to have their next battle, or on what date.

'There was a small island off the coast, little more than a rock really. All three clans claimed it was theirs. At one of their big meetings they decided that each clan would send a champion to the island on an appointed night. They would fight it out. The next morning, whichever clan's champion had won could claim the island.

'They chose their three champions and the three of them paddled out on small boats, all arriving just as the sun was setting. But the elders happened to have chosen three warriors who knew each other. In earlier, peaceful times, when they were just boys, the three of them had sailed as far as Iceland together and saved each others' lives many times.

132

'Instead of fighting they spent the whole night talking and began to realise that something strange was brewing. The fishermen of all the clans were unable to catch a single fish. They had all been reduced to living off seaweed. All three clans were starving but none had known that it was a problem they all shared. Then the trio discussed their disturbing dreams. They had all dreamed of the same beast.

'They did not even wait until morning, they made off to the coast where an old seer lived alone in a cave. They found her dying of starvation, having not been able to catch a fish in a long while. She told them the sea beast was only a day away. It was going to kill them all. They had come to her just in time. She told them what to do, and then she fell asleep and never woke up again.

'The next morning a large vessel with all the elders, statesmen and generals arrived to see who had won possession of the island. Instead they found the three desperate warriors. They wanted to take their boat and use it as a "signal of promise".'

'A signal of promise?' asked Ewan.

'That was what the seer told them to make,' said Weir, 'it was an ancient signal the beast was bound to obey.'

'Their leaders were persuaded to wait on the island while the trio loaded the boat with seaweed and went out to meet the beast. As darkness fell they set light to tar barrels and loaded the seaweed into them. The tall flames set light to their sails. The signal could be seen for many miles.

'As the beast raised its face, great waves threw them about, but they were strong boat handlers

133

and they stayed on course.

'The burning boat was an ancient signal. The beast sank back under waves and let the three clans live. They were given another chance. That was the power of the signal of promise. While rowing back to the island where they had left their leaders the trio came up with a further plan. They decided to leave their leaders there until they had made peace with each other.'

Weir laughed. He had become excited during his sermon. He was pacing back and forth across the deck.

'"We'll be back for you in a month," they shouted over to them, "you have a lot to talk about." It was a good plan. It worked. There began a time of peace on that coast.'

Weir smiled.

'The end.'

May frowned. Was Weir suggesting they use the *Sunny Buoy* to do the same thing?

'I have come across other stories like it,' Weir went on. 'The way I see it, you young people are the next generation of Ballydog. *You* can make the promise, face down the beast and save the town.'

Andrew was interested. Ballydog was his home.

Ewan was just as interested. He considered himself to have been forced from the city and did not want to run any more. Somewhere, deep in his personality, Ewan was glad to have found a way to prove himself.

'But we don't know when it is coming,' said May. 'We can't just sit out on the bay until it arrives.'

'It'll be at night though,' said Andrew, 'it's always after dark in my dreams.'

134

'Maybe that's because it's night when you're dreaming it,' said May.

'I get flashes of it during the day, too,' snapped Andrew, 'even if I close my eyes for just a few seconds.'

This silenced her. Weir nodded solemnly. 'The beast better come soon, or Andrew and myself may go completely mad . . . Yes, it will attack at night. Dozens of the legends mention night-time. Son, do you see the moon in your dreams about the beast?'

'I dunno, I don't pay much attention to the moon.'

'I have a theory the beast times its attack with the disappearing moon. It lives in the sea, with the tides, so it makes sense that it's influenced by the moon's phases. It certainly doesn't need to worry about predators but still it may instinctively attack under the cover of darkness. This would be one reason why it has left so few witnesses.'

'That it killed them all is a better reason,' said May.

'Yes, that too,' admitted Weir, 'but a few legends specifically mention that there was no moon shining on the night of the beast's arrival. I don't think that is a coincidence.'

'When is the next night of no moon, Mr Weir?' asked Ewan. Ewan did not believe in coincidence, either.

'A few nights from now,' Weir said.

The black night seemed to get blacker. Weir leaned back against the railing and looked towards the mouth of the bay, the mouth through which the beast would soon pass.

'So are you saying,' said Andrew, 'that on that

135

night we should go out on the *Sunny Buoy*, light a bonfire on deck and hope it won't attack?'

'If the description of the ritual in the tale is correct, then they burned dried seaweed and tar to produce as much light as possible. This is a very large beast. It simply will not *see* a signal that is too small. Still, we cannot set fire to your boat, or put a bonfire on it. We want to keep you as safe as we can. I have a different plan. We just produce *smoke* on the *Sunny Buoy* and get the light from elsewhere.'

* * *

Weir led them towards the lighthouse. Andrew and Ewan had walked this way together only a few nights before in an attempt to talk to him. Now they both followed, eager to see his demonstration. May trailed behind.

Down by the shore, within sight of the lighthouse, they came across an object planted in the ground. It was like a metre-tall orange candle.

'I left this here on my way down to see you,' said Weir. 'Do you know what it is?'

'Yeah, an emergency flare,' said Andrew. 'Pull the string and it burns so bright you can see it for miles.'

'That's right. But this one makes smoke, not light. It is for using during the day when a light flare could not be seen very well. But burning flares are not suitable for the plan because they don't stay lit for long and they are not very big. We can use the smoke flare to make something bigger, brighter and longer-lasting.'

Weir took a hold of the ripcord and prepared to

pull it.

'Better get back,' he said, 'the smoke is full of dye, it'll turn your clothes orange.'

Setting off the flare was like unbottling a cloud. With a *swoosh*, coloured smoke began pumping from the top. In no time the plume of smoke was six metres wide and the height of the lighthouse. From a short distance away Weir and the two boys watched it rise.

When the beam from the lighthouse swept around, Weir's plan suddenly became obvious. The beam lit up the smoke as if from the inside, it glowed bright and huge. The boys almost strained their necks looking up at the signal. The idea was simple but effective.

'I have made a reflector which I can place over the lighthouse light,' said Weir. 'I can use it to focus the beam and manoeuvre it so as to keep it trained on the *Sunny Buoy*. On the deck you can set off some smoke flares. I'll light up the smoke cloud. The beast will not miss you. The signal will be understood, loud and clear.'

Weir threw the flare into the sea and the cloud above dissipated. Andrew and Ewan considered the plan. Basically it was to chug out to the mouth of Ballydog Bay in a decrepit old trawler and broadcast themselves to a vast sea creature that exists mainly to destroy. The creature would realise Ballydog *showed promise* and go away.

It sounded impossible. Yet they liked the plan. It had a track record, at least if you believed in stories written centuries ago. And who was to say what was impossible? 'Impossible' did not mean much any more.

'What do you think?' Weir asked.

'It would be good to do *something*,' said Ewan. He wanted to take a stand. He would live up to the task of being chosen.

'Yeah,' Andrew agreed.

'May?'

May was unimpressed by the smoke and light show. 'Sorry,' she said, 'but I'm goin' to use the *Sunny Buoy* to get away. Ye'll have to find another boat to try your plan with. There're plenty over at the new pier, and ye can find skippers in The Lobster's Cage right now. Go ask them.'

Weir took a deep, disappointed breath. 'I understand you not wanting to risk your life over old stories. It's true, I can't guarantee you'll get back safe or that it will even work. But—'

'No,' said May. 'I think it could work fine. That's not the reason I won't do it.'

May looked in the direction of the fish finger factory. The Old Man of the Sea was there, and the taxidermist, right at that moment, was cutting him open. It was all she could think about. The leatherback's cold insides were being pulled out. His eyes scooped out and replaced with marbles. And as terrible as it was, this assault upon her friend was only the latest example of Ballydog's badness. May had known many others.

'I'm not risking me life for this town. I'm not even risking the *Sunny Buoy* for it, Ballydog has done nothing to deserve it. It's that simple.'

'Please,' said Andrew quietly. 'It might not be a great place but Ballydog is our home.'

'It's a wee bit late to start trying to make me feel at home now, Andrew.'

'Well, *I'm* at home!' he yelled. 'I've got a ma and da. I've got little brothers—'

'And what about your family, May?' asked Weir.

'I'll just have to talk me dad into leaving with me. Won't be easy, I know—'

'I wasn't thinking of him,' said Weir. 'What about the *other* member of your family?'

'There's only me and him.' May turned to face Weir. 'What are ye goin' on about?'

Weir shook his head sadly. 'It's not right that you hear this from me, but these are desperate times . . . I believe you have a special gift. Where do you suppose gifts like that come from? Out of thin air? No, they are in your genes, just like the colour of your eyes. But if you had a brother he would not have your kind of abilities. To be able to *see* the way you can is a talent for the female of the species only. Passed from mother to daughter, *grandmother to granddaughter . . .*'

'What do you mean?' May demanded.

'Years ago girls like yourself were burned at the stake. Even at your age. Nowadays you get rejected by society instead, especially a cruel one like Ballydog. Does that remind you of anyone?'

'Aye . . . maybe.'

'Your grandmother only ever had a son. No supernatural talents there. But he, *he* had a daughter. The problem was that he was disturbed by this mother. Just as much as every other person in Ballydog. He wanted to break the cycle. He kept his daughter and his mother apart, as if that could stop her talent growing and finding expression! But he knew the old folk would never tell you the truth, they love to keep secrets, and the younger people never knew the truth in the first place. I have given it away now and I am sorry you had to hear it from me. I hope you see why I had to do it.

139

The Woman on the Hill is your grandmother. She hasn't left her house in ten years and she never will again. If you want to save your family, all of them, then you'll have to save the whole town. It's *that* simple.'

CHAPTER TWENTY-ONE

May took a deep breath before pushing open the door. She stepped into the hot air, the thick yellow smell and the complete racket of the Lobster's Cage. She expected all the men to turn and stare at her, order her to get out, or laugh at her. In the end, none of the customers gave her much heed. She received a few stained grins from some of the drunken men but she was ignored by most. The drinkers were packed into the confines of the bar, holding pints of the yellow Ponny Dew tight up against their chests. There was a wild restraint about them all. They shouted but did not move, like angry dogs on leashes. There were women in the Lobster's Cage too, they had yellow fingers and, it seemed to May, they were laughing and crying at the same time. Everyone was yellow, more yellow than just the sickly lighting would explain. May realised her dad had this same yellow tint in his skin, even during the day. May was looking for him now. She was not as angry as she was entitled to be. Instead she was feeling off-balance and overloaded. May was like the Dimwheat that the Hunter had shown them during his visit. She had grown a lot in a very short time.

May pushed into the crowd. There were men

along the bar she did not think she had ever seen before. Not out on the street, not at Mass, not anywhere. Did they live in this bar? How long since they had seen the sun? Some leaned over and said things to her but she could not understand them. They grinned yellow grins and let her by.

May's dad was sitting alone at the far end of the bar, a pint of Ponny Dew before him. First he was shocked to see her, then embarrassed, then he tried to cover up his embarrassment.

'Come to visit your aul dad, eh?' he said. He extended his arms towards her waist, as if to lift her up and plop her on the stool next to him. But he stopped short. She was too old for that.

'Mineral?' he inquired. 'Crisps?'

'The Woman on the Hill, she's me grandma, ain't she?'

He looked down into his drink. He had known this would happen some day.

'Yes, your grandmother. My very own mother. That is her indeed.'

'Why didn't ye tell me?' May's voice was firm. She was nowhere near crying. This conversation was far too important for that.

'I wanted to protect you,' he said. 'Protect you from your history. The womanfolk of my family carry a curse. I thought if I kept you away from her influence and got doctors to come see you then we might be able to cure you.'

'They can't,' said May. 'Do you know why? Because I'm not sick. It's a talent.'

'Maybe,' said her father, wanting to appease her. 'Whatever it is I think it's dangerous. I just want you to be happy and I know being happy is

141

very hard for a person with your . . . talent. Look at your grandmother. You don't want to end up like her, do you? Rejected by the whole town?'

'Rejected by her own son,' said May.

'I bring her everything she needs once a week. Do you think it was easy for me when I was your age? I always looked after her. When I was a boy she would be struck by visions sometimes. Down the town, in the shop, or on the street, she would go still as a statue and stare off into space. I would have to take her home by the hand. It was unbearable. People can be cruel—'

'Ballydog people,' interrupted May.

'May,' he said sadly, 'do not kid yourself that Ballydog is so different from the rest of the world.'

May looked around at the bar. Everyone was talking, laughing, shouting, pretending, grasping, lying . . .

Her dad resumed. 'When I first married your mother we all lived in that cottage at the end of the Batter. You were born in the back bedroom and we lived there until you were a toddler. It was around that time your grandmother began refusing to leave the house. Me and your mother would take care of her, and she would babysit you sometimes when I went out fishing on the *Sunny Buoy*. But your mother couldn't take the life. The whispering and pointing in town, your grandmother's wild talk. That was the worst thing, her grabbing at people's hands and talking nonsense. I'm sorry, May, but it never did anybody any good. It may be a talent, it may be pure magic, but it never did anybody any good . . . One day I came back from fishing and your mother had packed and left. I've never seen nor heard from her since. You were two years old. It was then I became really determined to try and get you away from your grandmother and all that potential hurt. I wrapped you up in a blanket and we started spending our nights on the *Sunny Buoy*. It was not meant to be for ever, living on the boat, I mean. I'm sorry, things slipped away from me . . .'

He looked away.

'And what you feared most has happened in the end anyway,' said May. 'I'm still your mam's granddaughter, as sure as anything.'

'Yes you are,' he said, 'and yes, it's what I always feared.'

May looked around the bar. Underneath the racket and debate she thought she could hear the touch of fear in every voice that night. Maybe it was not only due to the approach of the sea creature. Maybe the fear had always been there. Then again, hadn't the sea creature always been approaching? May saw that Ballydog was not a community, it was just an unruly heap of people who happened to live in the same small place. It was constant war. A girl like May was bound to suffer more than most, but in reality they all were.

May looked at her dad. She loved him. She pitied him. She loved him.

'May,' he said, 'you will end up like your grandmother if you don't do something. You didn't need her to read your palm. Just by visiting her house and seeing how she lives you were seeing your own future.'

'Then I will do something,' she said, 'but not like you mean . . . I always thought my talent was a curse. Grandma said her talent was a curse too when I visited her. But I don't wanna live like that any more. That's the cycle I have to break. Talent is only a curse if ye don't use it.'

May slid off her stool.

Her father looked back across the bar. 'There's not much I can do for you,' he said.

'I've a couple of friends to help me,' said May.

Outside on the square Andrew and Ewan stood up as May approached them. She looked at the moon, it was a thin sliver. 'It's true. Turns out I have a grandmother,' she said.

'And . . . how is it?' asked Andrew.

'To have a grandmother?' added Ewan.

'Ye wanna know a funny thing?' she said. 'I always wanted one.'

She smiled, so they smiled.

'All right then so,' she said, 'we'll try and save the town.'

'Grand. I'm going to go right now and see what spare parts Weir has,' said Andrew.

'And I am going to the library,' said Ewan.

CHAPTER TWENTY-TWO

For years the *Sunny Buoy* was a dysfunctional place, a shipwreck waiting to happen. Now it was transformed into a place of activity and a symbol of *promise*. Andrew worked hard. Weir supplied replacement parts, including the cog they needed. Weir also brought them all hot meals. May was fascinated by Weir's cooking. It fired her senses. To May peppers were rare, garlic was exotic, ginger root was a thing she had never imagined. Weir laughed as he watched her trepidation quickly turn to enjoyment. As May handed back to Weir a stack of three licked-clean bowls, Weir took her by the arm. May was of slight build and Weir's thumb and forefinger made a ring around her arm easily.

'I'll have to fatten you up,' he said.

'Let's fix up the boat first,' she replied.

Soon the *Sunny Buoy* developed a noticeable shine. May's dad commented on it before going to work. 'Aren't you a great one sorting out the house for us?' he said to her, confused.

'Just getting it shipshape,' May told him.

If May's dad had lifted the cover off the engine he would have been shocked to discover the engine fit to run again. It positively gleamed.

A couple of nights later, May, Andrew and Ewan cheered as the ignition key turned and the engine roared into life. A vibration passed through the woodwork of the *Sunny Buoy* as it awakened from its long slumber. The youngsters were not cheering long. Immediately the wrinkled fan belt shredded and went to pieces, shooting threads of itself into the air. The engine's drive spun uselessly. Tantalised by having seen the engine fully functional for a few seconds, Ewan went straight to the lighthouse to ask Weir if he had a suitable fan belt among his gear.

Andrew felt awkward alone on the boat with May, but if Ewan returned directly with a fan belt Andrew could install it that very night, so he stayed. He sat on the deck and fiddled with a spanner pointlessly. May did not seem uncomfortable being alone with her former persecutor. She leaned on the railing and watched the thin moon, thinking mainly of her

145

grandmother. She had not been back to see her yet. There was work to do first.

'May,' Andrew said after five minutes of silence, 'I went into my brothers' room this morning and they'd made a giant monster using every single one of their building blocks. It gave me a fright.'

'Aye,' said May, 'other people are starting to feel the danger. Doubt they will understand what is happening until it is too late, though.'

'Yeah, you're probably right.'

There was silence for another while.

'May,' Andrew said, 'I'm really scared, I wish everything would just go away.'

'It's a scary thing,' said May, 'but ye know, and I'm not just trying to make ye jealous or anything, but I'm not one wee bit frightened. We might die, but for the first time in me life I'm not frightened at all.'

Ewan returned, bringing Weir with him.

'The fan belt gave out on us?' said Weir, pulling out a measuring tape. 'Those things always decay in time. I have none in my store but I will call a supplier right now to get him to send us one tomorrow. I just need to get a measurement. I'll need you to install it as soon as it arrives, son. We'll have no time to waste.'

'According to a moon calendar I found on the internet,' said Ewan, 'tomorrow night will be moonless, but so will nights after.'

'Yes, but we can be certain it attacks tomorrow night,' said Weir.

He quickly measured the distance from the cog to the driveshaft, and their respective diameters. Done, the measuring tape spun home with a *clack*.

'How do you know?' asked Ewan.

146

'I have noticed a theme in stories about the beast,' Weir said. 'With recent events in Ballydog it's become very obvious to me. Many places, on the very night of being claimed by the beast, had for themselves a kind of party. Sounds like madness, doesn't it? Well, I suppose madness is exactly what it is. Festivals, thrown for no apparent reason, are referred to in many of the legends. The people are afraid, but instead of facing their fear and trying to save themselves they try to ignore it. They have a party to help them ignore it. What's happening tomorrow night?'

'The moon will finally be gone?' said Ewan.

'The party in the fish finger factory,' said May, 'the unveiling of the stuffed Old Man, old leatherback I mean.'

'That's right,' said Weir, 'a moonless night and a festival combined, just as it is in at least a dozen stories. I believe the beast will attack tomorrow night.'

The three youngsters thought about it.

'I think you're right, Mr Weir,' said Ewan, 'everyone's nervous. People are only happy when they're talking about the party.'

'Aye,' said May, 'and the wilder the people of Ballydog get, the closer I think the monster must be. Deep down they all know something big is going to happen. It has already happened! Who could not worry about all the fish and animals disappearing?'

'Ballydog could,' said Andrew.

'Tomorrow night, then,' said Ewan.

'Tomorrow night, then so,' said May.

They turned to face the sea. It seemed more permanent than the town of Ballydog.

CHAPTER TWENTY-THREE

Long ago, during the days of the first prophets, on the island of Bolo, in the South China Sea, the Sultan called his chief advisor into his state room.

'Advisor,' said the Sultan, '. . . how do you feel today?'

The Advisor was caught off guard. The Sultan had never asked him anything personal before. He did not think the Sultan even knew his name. The Sultan was a snob, not interested in anyone whose social rank was too distant from his own. Furthermore, the Advisor was caught off guard because in truth he had not been feeling well lately. Bad dreams were ruining his sleep. He did not want the Sultan to know this; he did not want the Sultan to lose trust in his judgement. What good was an advisor without reliable judgement? An advisor without reliable judgment may as well be put to death.

'I feel better than I have ever done,' he said.

'Good, good,' said the Sultan, although he sounded disappointed. The Advisor noticed that the Sultan himself looked sickly. He had dark rings under his eyes.

'However, may I inform your High and Mightiness,' said the Advisor, 'unhappiness currently abounds on Bolo. The fishing has been extremely weak and some of your people are going hungry.'

'Do my people not all keep chickens for when the sea is lean?' the Sultan asked.

'There was a strange happening a few nights

ago. Most of the island's chickens took to their wings and left us. I doubt many of them managed to fly as far as other islands or to the mainland. Chickens are mainly fat and unused to flying, drowned chickens have been washing up on the beaches every day since. What possessed them to try and fly away we may never know. But the people are disturbed at such goings-on.'

'So am I,' said the Sultan. He adjusted his robes and looked around him nervously. 'Do you have any advice?'

'Yes, we should come together, as a people we so rarely come together. We could have prayers and a festival, perhaps the sacrifice of a cow or a pig? I know this may be distasteful to you but local gods are still powerful here. We should appease them. Perhaps this will fill our nets and calm our chickens.'

The Sultan thought this a good plan and bid it be so. The people were called upon to produce as much coconut wine as they could. They were glad to have something to do and set about preparing. Soon there began what was planned to be three days of festivities. The people of Bolo roasted all the chickens that had not flown away, and a few of those that washed up on the shore. They were okay to eat, just a little salty. They drank the frothy wine, hugged and danced. It was a very emotional day. A cow was painted up for slaughter.

The Sultan had made many enemies of neighbouring sultanates but that evening he was filled with a sudden goodwill and a desire for friendship.

'Advisor,' he said, 'send out invitations to all the nearest sultans to come join our festival.

Guarantee them safe passage.'

The Advisor left with a courtly bow. Right outside the door he met a boy called Ali. The Advisor ordered him to find a canoe and take the message to one island a little to the west. Then the Advisor went off looking for more boys to take the message to other islands, but he became distracted. The ritual killing of the cow was about to begin. He was drawn towards it.

It was a loud pulsing ritual. Dancing, chanting, the clacking of hundreds of bamboo sticks. Everyone on the island had converted to Islam in the last generation or two but that night older gods were re-emerging. The Advisor and everyone else were lost in the event. They danced, drank and spun each other around under a moonless sky.

The sultan of the neighbouring island was delighted when Ali arrived and made the invitation. He would certainly attend the festival, but tomorrow as it was already very late and the sea was becoming rough. Ali stayed there with them as it did indeed appear a storm was blowing in.

The next morning the sea was calm again. Ali travelled with the other sultan and his retinue. They headed for Bolo on their brightly-coloured catamarans, but they could not find Bolo. There was nothing but shattered coral reef for kilometres in all directions. The entire island and everyone on it was gone.

The Advisor had sent away no one but Ali. He was the only survivor of Bolo. He became a drifter, spending much of the rest of his life canoeing from island to island. He told the story of Bolo to anyone who would listen.

'A whole island! Vanished,' he would tell people.

'A giant hand from the sky did it, I think, grabbed it out of the sea.'

A crazy story, but Ali was not completely wrong.

That night the people of Bolo, with agitated spirits but full bellies, had fallen into deep sleeps. Many did not make it back to their homes but lay on the beaches or under the palms. Then the sea creature rose, torrents of water crashing off its body. It scooped up the island in its maw, taking about three hours to completely erase it. The people who woke and witnessed the end of Bolo thought they had died and gone to hell.

Neither were they completely wrong.

CHAPTER TWENTY-FOUR

Mr and Mrs Trim closed their playschool early the next day. They were distressed. They had handed out paper and finger-paint then told the little boys to paint trawlers and the little girls to paint houses. That boys paint boats and girls paint houses had always been the rule in their playschool. They were preparing the children for their future roles in Ballydog: fishermen and housewives.

The children did not do as they were told. They could not have even if they wanted to. Every child fell silent and painted a sea monster. It was the same monster in all their pictures, although painted in very different styles and colours. It seemed to be a gigantic centipede, with circles on stalks for eyes and a mop of tongues.

In pictures painted by boys, the monster was eating fleets of trawlers. In pictures painted by

151

girls, it was eating rows of houses.

The pictures sent sharp shivers up Mrs Trim's spine. Mr Trim broke out in a sweat, something he had never done before. Sternly, they sent all the children home early.

'At least there is the party to look forward to tonight, Mrs Trim,' said Mr Trim as they burned the pictures in their fireplace.

'True,' said Mrs Trim. 'I shall take the opportunity to tell certain parents not to allow their offspring to watch horror films. They go straight to their heads.'

*   *   *

Heiferon was drumming his fingers on his desk. The classroom was a chaos of backchat and flying objects. With the excitement of tonight's party in the factory to look forward to there was no way he was going to get the class to settle down.

'Is May with her head-doctor today?' he barked at a student near the front.

'Don't think so,' she said.

'Maybe she is off with her boyfriend, the Northboy,' said Cynthia, 'he's absent too.'

'Andrew didn't turn up today, either,' said Mushroom. 'Wonder where he is?'

*   *   *

Mr Weir listened to the weather forecast for the night on his portable radio, cold but calm. He was on the platform on top of the lighthouse, in the open air by the light. The platform was about a metre wide and ran all the way around the light's casing. It was ringed by a low guard rail. Weir unscrewed the casing and installed what he called the Beamer. Carefully he slotted it over the light, it fitted snugly. The Beamer looked like a giant light bulb itself, but of steel not glass. The round end fitted over the light and funnelled it so Weir could focus the beam and point it wherever he wished. He had constructed the Beamer himself. Cut and polished the steel, welded it all together. He had tested it already, late one night, a week before, while Ballydog slept. No one had seen the light stop pulsing and point instead, like a headlight, onto a patch of the bay.

When he finished his work, Mr Weir drank a mug of tea and looked out over the bay. He would save it, it was his divine mission. He felt a powerful, but brief, surge of guilt for how he was using May, Ewan and Andrew. It was like a rumble, but in his heart not his stomach. Still, Weir believed the ends justified the means. Tonight the youngsters will face the beast and he will watch. Mr Weir always knew it was a cruel world.

*   *   *

The lower panels of Mrs Hooard's van scraped the ground as she pulled into the town square. It was carrying an unusually heavy load. This was nothing to do with the weight of the fan belt. That was a small package. It was on the front passenger seat and Hooard handed it to the three youngsters before going to open the back of the van. Andrew ripped open the plastic packaging right there and examined the fan belt.

The great weight was a large steel case, bound

153

in steel straps and combination locked. It looked like trouble. It stood in the back, between the axles of the van. It was dented and cruel-looking; words in a foreign alphabet were stamped into it. It seemed to belong in a war zone. 'Mr Teodors, room seven, care of the Ballydog Hotel,' was written on its label.

Mr Boyle arrived, pushing a trolley. 'That'll be a great party we'll have the night,' he said to Mrs Hooard, 'you'll be there?'

'I will,' she said.

'I hear you've something for my customer, Mr Teodors.'

'That's it there,' said Hooard, 'get it out of my sight.'

Mr Boyle's jaw dropped at the size of the steel case.

'I should've sent him over to get this himself,' he said. 'I could do my back in.'

'*You* should quit your complaining,' said Hooard, 'he's the first customer you've had in months. Be grateful.'

'He's not taking this thing into his room, that's for sure,' said Mr Boyle. 'He can store it in the garage. I'll charge him extra for it. It's big enough to count as a guest.'

Andrew, May and Ewan were already in the hotel. They had seen the case and read its label. The reception desk was unattended; Mrs Boyle was out the back painting her fingernails. They went straight up the stairs to room seven.

May knocked hard. The door opened just a fraction and the Hunter peered out.

'Ya! Hello, my young friends.'

He did not seem to register their angry

154

expressions. There was a long thin cigar between his teeth, sending smoke out into the hall through the narrow gap.

'We told ye to go, why are ye still here?' May demanded.

He drew the cigar out of his mouth. 'Monsters are my business, I hear one is coming so I stay to get a look at it. Call it research. I am certainly not here for fun, I mean . . .' his nose wrinkled, 'this is not a very nice town, is it?'

'We're taking care of the creature ourselves and we don't want ye causing trouble,' May said. 'We don't want ye flying around setting off bombs. What's in the metal box that's arrived for ye?'

The Hunter laughed. 'Don't worry. It's salamander's plasma for my jetpack. I used all I had to get here. It is not a bomb, although I would not recommend putting a match to it!'

They did not know whether to believe him or not. Would a nuclear warhead fit in that metal chest? Would the Hunter attempt to kill the creature despite not being paid, in the name of research?

'Now you've got your plasma ye can fly right out of here,' said May, furious. 'Go on, get PACKING!' She kicked at the door. The Hunter was holding it stiffly, the gap did not widen.

'Behave yourself, little girl,' said the Hunter. 'I know I could go now, but things are getting interesting. I stay a while. I will do no harm, maybe I can help you. What is your plan?'

Despite May's anger, Ewan could see no harm in telling the Hunter what they had learned and what they were going to do. Explaining their plan to him might dissuade him from doing anything

155

too . . . explosive. Ewan told him about Mr Weir's studies and 'the signal of promise.' The Hunter listened closely, then asked: 'Who will pilot this boat?'

'We will.'

'Brave.' The Hunter was impressed. He took a drag of his cigar. 'But I am not sure about this plan. You say your friend, the lighthouse man, has studied the monster but I have studied much also and have never heard of a monster accepting promises and going home. Monsters have to destroy. That is what they do. That is what makes them monsters and not mammals.'

'Yeah, well, it's the only plan we've got,' said Andrew.

'I have a suggestion,' said the Hunter, 'just escape. That's what I will do when the monster gets to town, but I have my jetpack, you just have legs. You will need to start running early.'

'We've decided to stay,' said Ewan. 'We believe we've been chosen.'

That remark made both Andrew and May look at Ewan with their eyebrows raised. He had started talking like Weir.

The Hunter thumped his chest. He was a sucker for bravery, 'I tell you what I will do. I will contact a few people, connections of mine in the business. I will ask them about this "signal of promise". Call it research.'

'Okay,' said Ewan. 'Come to the old pier and tell us if you discover anything.'

'He won't tell us anything worth knowing,' said May, 'he's only trouble.'

'Rude little girl,' said the Hunter. 'I can already tell you one thing, the monster is very close —'

156

'It arrives tonight,' said Andrew, 'we're sure of it.'

'Ya, that fits,' said the Hunter. 'Have a look what the Dimwheat says.'

With that he threw his door open wide. A warm organic smell hit the three youngsters. The room was almost entirely occupied by the Dimwheat. The seedling they saw germinate on the night of the Hunter's arrival had continued growing. Thick green vines climbed the walls and clung to the roof. Fat lush leaves hung from them. It was a jungle in there. The actual room could hardly be seen. The Hunter kept hacking away sections so he could move about but there was barely any free space left. Vines wrapped around the furniture, choking and cracking the wood. The bed was raised off the ground by the vegetation swarming beneath it. The Hunter had drawn his curtains tight but it would not be long until the plant burst out of the window to invade the street below. Mr Boyle would not be happy.

The youngsters were stunned. Even as they watched, new leaves were unrolling. The plant murmured and rustled with growth. The Hunter smiled broadly at them, and raised his arms as if to say, *tah-dah*. He was enjoying this. He leaned over until his face was close to May's and he said, 'Are you frightened yet, little girl?'

'NO.'

Disappointment flickered across the Hunter's face. 'You will be,' he said.

CHAPTER TWENTY-FIVE

Ewan tried to distract May from watching the fish finger factory. The people of Ballydog were gathering around it and going inside. They were all in their Sunday best. A banner had been hung across the factory's entrance. Everything could be seen from the deck of the *Sunny Buoy*. The people's excited babble carried across the water.

'Try and ignore them,' he told her, 'they don't know what they're doing.'

White anger burned behind May's eyes.

The problem was, there was nothing to do now but wait until dark. They had tied a dozen smoke flares to the mast. They had glued a seal around the engine covering and made it watertight. The fuel tank was filled and the engine tuned. Andrew needed only a few minutes to fit the fan belt and bring it up to full tension. Now he was standing on the end of the pier, looking out over the calm water.

Ewan and May don't need me any more, he was thinking. *I could run away.*

*   *   *

Two hundred kilometres away, an ocean swell was moving towards Ballydog. Beneath it, the creature was marching. The forgotten wreck of HMS *Reliant* was pulverised as the creature, too impatient to go around it, tore through it instead.

*   *   *

The party in the fish finger factory was warming up. Soon everyone would be there. The Ballydog Bangers, the local three-piece band, were performing waltzes, jigs and Elton John songs, out of key and too fast. The people danced, drank and discussed the tourist trade soon arriving and making them rich. Conn McKann was busy pouring Ponny Dew into everyone's glasses. The floor was soon wet and yellow with spilt drink.

'Keep it pouring,' Fitz said to him with a wink.

Standing over them, waiting to be unveiled, a square tent occupied the middle of the factory. It hid the leatherback turtle's glass case, the centrepiece of the evening's celebrations. The woman from *Guinness World Records* was due to visit and measure the turtle in a few days. Her visit would make it an official record-breaker. Fitz stood beside the sheet, keeping the young kids from peeping under it. The unveiling of the turtle would be his job. He smiled to himself as he watched the simple townsfolk enjoying themselves. He loved them in his way. They were his people.

As darkness fell, the crowd got wilder. Mr Fuller, the taxidermist, was sampling Ponny Dew and politely claimed to like it.

'And I've got something for you,' said Fuller. He wheeled out a vat of bubbling stew. He had prepared it in a stainless-steel container, the size of a bathtub, where the additives for the fish fingers had once been blended. He stirred the hot green stew with the biggest ladle he could find and threw in big handfuls of salt.

'Line up for a dish of turtle stew!' he called. Many people gathered around the vat and sniffed at it. Fuller ladled stew into polystyrene bowls and passed them around to those eager to try it, which was plenty. 'Delicious,' the people of Ballydog proclaimed, as rivulets of stew ran down their chins.

'Even better than sausage rolls,' said Patsy Leary.

'You must give me the recipe,' said Mrs Lynch.

The band played faster. Voices were raised and stayed raised. Men and women danced wildly. The teenagers gossiped and moved around in gangs. The children ran and chased each other. Bowls of stew were gobbled down.

Fitz lifted his arms and gradually the crowd quietened. The Ballydog Bangers shuddered to a halt. But the factory was still far from silent, there was a hum of nervous excitement that could have been heard across the square.

'Ladies and gentlemen, thanks for coming,' spoke Fitz into his microphone. Through the amplifier his voice was made large and reached every corner of the factory. 'It's wonderful to see you all coming together like this. I'm not going to frustrate you with too many words right now. I reckon I'll let this giant do the talking. It's time to see what has brought us all together.'

The crowd moved closer to the covered case. Fitz took a corner of the sheet in this fist.

'My gift to you!' The sheet came off with a flourish. The people pushed in, elbowing each other for a better view of the catch. Those in front pressed their faces right against the glass. The turtle looked back at them with false eyes. Thousands of stitches held his body together, but they criss-crossed his underbelly and were mainly

160

hidden from view. His shell had been varnished. His insides had been taken out, made into stew, and replaced with sawdust. His flippers were bent upward in a cruel imitation of swimming. The Old Man of the Sea was no longer a real leatherback. He was the impersonation of a leatherback. An impersonation constructed from his own corpse.

The people released a cheer that sounded like a scream. It was piercing, long and loud. It echoed up the factory's chimney and down the lanes of Ballydog. It carried across the water and crawled under May's skin. She could not stop herself. She ran towards the source of that inhuman shriek.

'May, come back!' Ewan called to her.

She did not stop. Ewan looked to Andrew but he only shrugged. Andrew did not know what to do with girls in tantrums.

May ran along the shore and across the town square to the looming factory. Outside, Mushroom and MacPherson were drinking Ponny Dew out of plastic cups. They saw her and shouted abuse.

Inside, people were walking around the tourist attraction, reaching out and touching the case like it contained a holy relic.

'This is a great day for Ballydog,' Fitz was saying into the microphone. 'A new beginning.'

They all knew he was right. His audience was rapt in intense devotion. A powerful sense of relief flowed through the people of Ballydog. Some openly cried.

When May entered and saw the turtle she automatically moved towards him. She saw and smelled the stew but did not realise what it was. The crowd paid no attention to her at all. They were hanging on Fitz's every word. It was shaping

161

up to be Fitz's best speech ever, but May could barely hear it. She walked up to the turtle. Dead eyes looked back at her. She put her forehead against the glass of his case. A few tears came loose but her chin held firm. A few moments later a hand rested on her shoulder. It was Ewan. He had run after her.

'We have to go,' he was saying. 'Please,' he was saying.

Ewan was painfully aware that darkness was falling. Stars were beginning to glimmer in the moonless sky. May seemed to have forgotten the job they had to do. Slowly, gently, he removed her from the case and led her back towards the entrance. She bowed her head and went.

'Our community has had a hard time lately,' Fitz's voice boomed. 'We deserve better, now we've got it.'

May stopped.

She spun around and bolted towards Fitz. Ewan was left grasping the air where she had been. She shoved people out of the way as she charged through the crowd. Ponny Dew and turtle stew flew out of people's hands. They objected loudly. Had the weirdo finally flipped completely? In front of Fitz she jumped. Her feet left the ground and she flung a punch, catching him neatly under the chin, which sent him staggering backwards. She landed, fell over, stood up and turned on the audience. They were all frozen by the shock of May's attack. They looked like characters in a cheap cartoon, their blinking eyes the only part of them that moved. They were May's now. She needed no microphone.

'Talking about community? None of ye care less

about community! The only time ye get together is when you're frightened. And then is it to do anything about your fear? No, it is to dance around this dead thing. An animal ye killed so ye could dance around it! This whole place deserves to be TAKEN! Ripped out OF THE GROUND. And ye LOT . . .'

May pointed around the room. The crowd cowered as if her finger were a magic wand, able to unleash punishments.

'Ye lot should go home and hide under your beds with shame!'

May stopped. She was breathing hard. More quietly she said, ' "Divided we fall," that's the expression, ain't it? But it's not always true. Ballydog is in pieces but still won't fall. It just goes on and on, not quite falling but never standing either. Not doing anything but harm. Tonight Ballydog might finally fall or it might not. The best thing ye can all do now is go home. Ye should all just go home, hide and hope ye'll be spared.'

The crowd was silent.

'May, we better go,' said Ewan. He took her by the hand. She allowed herself to be led. They walked slow at first, then faster. The crowd parted to let them through. They had broken into a run before reaching the outside.

'How was that for a speech?' May called as they left.

'That's right, clear out,' Fitz shouted, but May and Ewan were already out of earshot. He pulled at the neck of his jumper. He hoped the crowd would join him in shouting at the youngsters, but they did not. Clearly bothered, Fitz searched around for the microphone. He picked it up but it no longer worked.

'Stupid thing . . . still, no matter. Don't reckon I need it. Where was I? . . . Savage? Are you all right?'

Captain Savage of the *Ravenous Rachel* had fallen against a wall, he was distinctly green around the gills.

'I don't know, Mr Fitzpatrick,' he said, 'I feel poorly all of a sudden.'

'It was that stew I'd say. I'd better get you home,' said his wife, but it was obvious she was glad of the excuse to leave.

Other people were heading for the door as well.

'Hey, where are you going? We're only getting started,' said Fitz, laughing but angry.

'We're not feeling so good either,' the Toil brothers murmured. 'Think we'll go home.'

'You're not letting that weirdo bother you, are you?' demanded Fitz.

'No, of course not,' insisted Mrs Gin, who was also leaving. Her voice was strangely subdued, 'That stew was terribly rich. I need to go under my bed . . . sorry . . . go *to* my bed.'

'Yes, and we don't like being out too late,' said Mr and Mrs Trim.

Other people were creeping out the back way. Children were being led away by their parents. The band packed up their instruments.

'I feel a little *quare* too, Mr Fitzpatrick,' said Heiferon, with a strained laugh. 'But there's no need to overdo it tonight. We have the summer to look forward to!'

Heiferon looked around at the dwindling crowd for reassurance. *There would be a summer, wouldn't there?*

164

Kilfeather hadn't taken any stew but he felt ill nonetheless. He decided he simply had to go home right then and do his taxes, properly this time. Father Fingers felt the urge to pray. Despite the cold Mr Boyle found that he had broken out into a sweat. *Must be food poisoning*, he decided. 'I will take to my bed for a day or two,' he told his wife as they hurried across the square.

Everyone was abandoning the fish finger factory. Within half an hour everyone was gone. A few had slipped into the Lobster's Cage where McKann locked the door and told them they could drink all they liked. 'But I'm going home,' he said.

The people of Ballydog locked their doors, drew their curtains, pulled down their blinds. Some made strong cups of tea, some got in their beds, others hid under them. They felt anxious, sick, but above all, they felt doomed.

On the way back to the old pier May faltered at the junction leading out of town. She looked up to where the road disappeared over the hill. May knew that somewhere beyond Ballydog were better places. All she had to do was start walking. By dawn she would be in kinder country. If she had been alone then she may have done just that, started walking inland and left Ballydog to its fate. But she was not alone, Ewan was with her and he was not for running. Now was the time. The Big Facing Up To Things. They returned to the *Sunny Buoy*.

When May and Ewan got back they discovered it was Andrew who had run away.

CHAPTER TWENTY-SIX

It was true that Andrew had abandoned the *Sunny Buoy*, but all was not quite as it seemed.

Mushroom and MacPherson had been watching the townsfolk arriving at the factory. They had seen May run into the factory. Two minutes later they saw the Northboy going in after her.

'Maybe they've had a tiff,' said Mushroom. His voice was slurred. They had stayed outside so they could secretly drink Ponny Dew. They kept their plastic cups out of sight, but not many of the adults would have stopped them drinking Ponny Dew. The boys were thirteen now, and tonight was a special night. Let them have a little drink they would have said, let them get used to it.

'Say, now those two are at the party I bet you a tenner Andrew is alone on the *Sunny Buoy*.'

'Gru-of,' said MacPherson.

'Yeah, let's go look.'

They took deep slugs to empty their cups, tossed them away and set off towards the old pier. 'What will we do to him if we catch him?' wondered Mushroom aloud.

'Wannn ack boo ee crang ki assa bong-gritt!' said MacPherson.

'Tonne!' said Mushroom. 'And some people say you have no imagination.'

*   *   *

Andrew was at the bow of the boat. His mind could barely accept what his eyes saw. Yet it was really happening; the tide, which had begun going out only an hour before, was coming back in again. He watched the water level rising against the stone of the old pier. The water was not rough, the opposite in fact, it was a still night and the bay was a deathly calm, but the tide was rising when it should have been falling.

More than Andrew ever wanted anything; he wanted it to be tomorrow already.

He took deep breaths to calm himself. There was a thumping he could feel in his knees. He thought it was the sound of his own frightened heart, and he placed his hand over it. But it was not his heart, it was Tonne MacPherson's feet stomping across the deck.

MacPherson grabbed Andrew's shoulders and threw him against the mast of the *Sunny Buoy*. The flares tied to the top rattled in unison. Mushroom stepped aboard, kicked at the boat's woodwork and snorted.

'You gave up The Villa for this kip?'

'It's got sea views,' said Andrew.

MacPherson aimed a punch at Andrew's face but delivered it too slow. Andrew dipped his head sideways and MacPherson's fist struck the mast and it vibrated again. MacPherson grabbed his injured fingers and made a long whining noise.

'Ooooh, all you've done now is make him angry,' said Mushroom.

Andrew had no chance. Running was his only option.

He broke between the two boys but Mushroom tripped him up. Andrew hit the deck and the next thing he felt was MacPherson's hands clamped around his ankles. He was dragged back along the deck. He tried to grab at the railings, at Mushroom, at anything but MacPherson was beginning to spin him around. Andrew fought to protect his head and upper body as he was spun in a complete revolution.

Mushroom was delighted. 'MAN OVER-BOARD,' he howled.

MacPherson released Andrew's ankles and he spun through the air. Water and sky swapped positions several times. Then Andrew was in the water. He broke the surface and swam for shore. This was not exactly how he had wanted it but at least he was away from the boys.

Ponny Dew was also on his side. Suddenly ill from having spun around, MacPherson collapsed, pulled himself to his knees and vomited a yellow stream over the side. Mushroom was not to be overpowered by the Ponny Dew yet, even though he had drunk as much as MacPherson. His hatred of Andrew kept him going.

'Get up, you big lump, we have to catch him,' he said.

'Gee iraa elf!'

Andrew struggled ashore. He clambered over the rocks onto the path. He ran in the direction of the lighthouse. MacPherson staggered after him, driven on by Mushroom. Andrew's clothes were heavy with seawater and slowed him down. On a rise he paused a moment, panting heavily. He could see the top of the lighthouse from there. Its light had come on but was not revolving. It shone in one direction only, angled slightly downward so that it hit the surface of the bay and made an oval of light. It was hard to be sure but Andrew thought he could see Weir's silhouette up on the platform by the Beamer. No doubt he was wondering why the *Sunny Buoy* had not set out yet.

'Come here till we bust you,' Mushroom yelled. They were still after him.

Andrew left the path and clambered up a rushy slope. The ground was soft and clung at his feet.

'Gotta, getta, way,' he kept repeating under his breath as he fought onwards.

MacPherson emitted a complaining howl. With his big feet and sore head he was finding the going extremely difficult. It sounded as if they were falling behind. Andrew ran on some more before allowing himself to stop and look back. MacPherson had collapsed into the rushes and Mushroom could not budge him.

'Get up, GET UP!'

Feeling safer, Andrew walked further before sitting heavily down where he could keep an eye on his two pursuers. His chest heaved in and out and his breath, the little he had, hurt his throat. Mushroom had also fallen down alongside MacPherson and they were both silent. Could it be a trick? Andrew waited two minutes.

As he waited he noticed another strange phenomenon in the bay to go along with the rising tide. The water was calm but moving across it, presumably originating from out on the open sea, was one solitary high wave. Andrew could see it clearly as it passed through the spot of the lighthouse. Then it crashed loudly against the shore.

Best to wait another minute or two, Andrew decided, *don't want to lead Mushroom and MacPherson back to the Sunny Buoy. That might ruin the plan.*

Five minutes later another wave entered the bay and hit the shore. Andrew watched it arrive from his place among the rushes. He could feel his clothes drying against his skin. A breeze was beginning to come off the sea. Down the slope, MacPherson began snoring.

Another minute, thought Andrew. Just to be on the safe side.

Five minutes later he was still there.

By now Andrew knew what he was doing. He was abandoning his friends.

*   *   *

Fifty kilometres out to sea the top of the vast sea creature broke the surface of the Atlantic and went under again. It was as if an island was raised and, as quickly, sunk. Below, the creature's progress was reshaping the seabed.

*   *   *

Andrew heard a chugging sound on the breeze, an old tractor engine. The *Sunny Buoy* came into view. Under the mast-light he could see Ewan checking the smoke flares. May must have been in the wheelhouse, steering the boat towards the mouth of the bay. From the top of the lighthouse, Weir aimed the Beamer upon the trawler. The boat was small in the dark night but somehow splendid. The focused attention of the light marked it as special. A brave, glowing thing.

Andrew felt proud to have got the *Sunny Buoy* running again. It was the first time it had moved in ten years. Then he felt ashamed that he was not on

170

it. He should have been at the bow right then, leaning into the breeze, instead of watching from a distance. He thought about right, he thought about wrong. It left him with a sore heart. Andrew felt something he had never felt before. Something he could have never imagined before. He was Sorry.

Andrew sank back into the rushes. He would have liked to keep sinking.

The *Sunny Buoy* was lifted on a wave and slid down the other side, all the while aimed directly towards the mouth of the bay. It was making good progress. Andrew watched it go.

Then, sudden like a shooting star, a scorching arc of pinkish heat was drawn over Ballydog. The Hunter was on the move again. *Probably getting out of town*, thought Andrew, but actually the Hunter was flying towards the lighthouse. He flew not far above Andrew's head and, although the Hunter did not see the boy in the rushes, Andrew saw him clearly. There was a determined angle to the Hunter's jaw. His free hand was in a tight fist and extended out in front of him. *He really thinks he is Superman*, thought Andrew. The Hunter slowed as he neared the lighthouse and dropped into a vertical position. Andrew wondered what the Hunter was doing. He remembered the warning prediction May's grandmother had given her. He had not taken it too seriously at the time, but now . . . Andrew set off towards the lighthouse. He kept an eye on Mushroom and MacPherson but they were both deeply asleep at that stage. Ponny Dew had got the better of them.

The Hunter crashed through the lowest window of the lighthouse, splintering it into pieces. He cut the plasma stream at the last moment and fell into

Weir's first-floor room. From the top of the lighthouse Weir did not see or hear the Hunter's dramatic entry. Weir was giving his full attention to the light, keeping the beam trained on the *Sunny Buoy*. The boat was getting smaller every minute.

Then the *Sunny Buoy* vanished into blackness. The light had been cut.

Andrew started running. He had no doubt who was responsible. The Hunter had cut the light via the automation unit on the wall of the first-floor room.

Above, Weir tore open the trapdoor in the platform and slid down the ladder.

'Weir!' Andrew shouted. 'Be careful—'

Weir had not heard him. Andrew's shout was lost to the distance and the breeze. Weir probably thought it was a technical problem he was going to have to fix. He would get a surprise when he found a Latvian in a jetpack standing in his living room. Andrew ran, leaping the rushes and half-tumbling to the door of the lighthouse. He knew the Hunter was armed and feared the worst for Weir. What did the Hunter want? Why had he sabotaged their attempt to save the town? The *Sunny Buoy* was now lost in darkness, its mast-light just a tiny pinpoint no gigantic creature would register. No promise-signal would be sent, and as the creature bore down on Ballydog, the *Sunny Buoy* and its crew would probably be crushed.

The door of the lighthouse was locked. Andrew threw himself against it, but it was as solid as the wall it was set in.

Weir took the steps five at a time. He flung himself downwards into the room. The Hunter was examining the contents of the automation box. He

172

had wrenched it open and pulled at levers randomly until the light had been killed. Weir was too frenzied and driven to be surprised by even the strange sight of this super-equipped man. For weeks Weir had honed his plan. He had read the manuscripts, done the research, he had schemed and plotted late into each night. Against all odds he had found a boat and a crew. No one was going to stop him now. Weir hardly even saw the man in the jetpack. He only saw a problem to be removed immediately.

So it was the Hunter who was surprised by the alarmingly tall man charging at him like a demon. When Weir rushed him he lost his balance and careered backwards, falling against the window frame that he had passed through less than a minute before. The weight of the jetpack, recently refilled with fuel, tugged at him. He fought gravity to stop himself falling out. Then Weir had his legs.

'Get off my property,' Weir said as he tossed the intruder out of the window.

The Hunter hit the ground with a loud crack. He thought he had probably broken some piece of equipment. He was correct, it was his right arm, broken in two places. Pain activated his tear ducts. As if that was not enough, someone began kicking and swearing at him. It was Andrew.

'What do you think you're doing? The light's gone, the thing won't see them. You've wrecked everything!'

The Hunter raised his good arm in an attempt to protect himself. 'I did it to save them,' he protested. 'I should have known there was no such thing as making promises to a monster. It's not true what the lighthouse man told you. I talked

173

with some contacts and worked out what he is doing. A sacrifice! *That* is his real plan. He is sacrificing them to appease the monster. Just like people have done for centuries. He has sent them to their deaths.'

'But May's grandma warned her about you,' said Andrew. 'She said someone would use her for his own ends, someone who would come down . . . *from . . .*'

Andrew turned his face upwards and his words trailed away. The sheer white surface of the lighthouse extended thirty-five metres into the air.

'on . . . high.'

Just then the light beamed out again. Weir had reconnected it. The *Sunny Buoy*, rising and falling on tall swells, was exposed once more.

CHAPTER TWENTY-SEVEN

'I hope you've brought some food,' was the first thing the seer said to the three warriors when they arrived at her cave, 'I'm starved.'

The heroes of the three clans had almost nothing themselves, just a couple of pieces of dried seaweed. The food revived her a little but she was a very old woman and to go so long without eating was more than her body could take.

'Seer,' they implored, 'we have been distracted by our wars for so long but now our hearts tell us a giant approaches, is it true?'

'Your hearts have it right,' she said. She had to be assisted so that she could sit up on the sand at the mouth of her cave. 'Tomorrow night will be the

174

end of us. The biggest fury in the world has awoken and it will not be easy to satisfy, not without our elimination.'

'But it *can* be satisfied in another way?'

'I believe it can, yes. You will need a volunteer. Whether they actually volunteer or not is up to you. Make a sacrifice, a human sacrifice. That may appease it.'

'But it's so huge,' said one of the men, 'we've seen it in dreams. Will it take just one human life as a sacrifice?'

With a stick-like finger she slowly drew an image in the sand: a boat with a person standing by the mast. She grimaced painfully as she drew, these were her last reserves of strength. When she was done she looked at it for a while.

'Hmmm.'

She drew more people on the deck.

'I would give it a few extra just to be sure,' she said, 'and be certain you mark your sacrifice. Light it up, make it tall with flame, and send it out to meet its fate.'

She added flames to the boat.

'That is how the sea creature will know you understand its greatness. You must show respect to its size, you must show that it has humbled you.'

With a slow sweep she drew a circle around the boat, the sea creature's mouth. 'But you must give it human blood. Remember, it's not an animal, it's a monster,' she said.

She scrubbed out the image with her hand.

'Now, let me sleep,' she said.

*　　　*　　　*

175

As planned, the elders arrived in a boat at the contested rock the next morning to see who had won it. But they found themselves under attack by the three heroes, each of them as alive as the other. Some fought back but were quickly despatched. The rest submitted and allowed themselves to be tied up along the sides of the boat. Twenty-two men and women were captured, some of the highest ranking members of each of the three clans.

The elders were tied up in no particular order, the clans were mixed, and they spent the whole day whispering together while the three heroes prepared barrels of tar and collected seaweed. As darkness approached, the leaders called to their captors.

'Your actions have made us see sense,' they said, 'we are prepared to make peace.'

The three men looked at one another and shrugged. It was too late now.

*   *   *

That was the real legend. The burning boat was sent out, with its cargo of people. The pitiful sound of the elders' moaning and crying blended with the wind and eventually disappeared into it. The creature, a living hole in the world, emerged from the sea. It fell upon the sacrifice, accepted and swallowed it. Then it disappeared back into the North Sea. The creature could be appeased in only one way: a sacrifice, a human sacrifice. The 'signal of promise' was an invention: Weir's invention. His true plan was to make a sacrificial offering to the beast. May and Ewan were going to be that sacrifice.

CHAPTER TWENTY-EIGHT

Right then, the *Sunny Buoy* was being dragged up
on the crest of a swell. Each wave that hit them
was taller than the last. Clinging on to the wheel,
May kept the bow pointed directly into them. If a
swell was allowed to hit them side-on they would
be capsized. They were almost at the mouth of the
bay and exposed to the open ocean. The *Sunny
Buoy* creaked and banged with the rising and
falling of the boat, the grinding of its old boards
sounding like one hundred old doors creaking
open, slamming shut and creaking opening again.

Ewan's arms were wrapped around the mast.
Salt water slapped his face at every gust. From
there at the mast he could grab the ripcords of all
the flares at a moment's notice. One sharp tug and
they would all go off together.

The face of the creature was twenty kilometres
away, entering the shallower sea of the coast. Soon
it would surface.

It was then that the light was cut. May, Ewan
and the *Sunny Buoy* were left alone in the night.

'What's goin' on?' May yelled.

Hand over hand along the railing, Ewan moved
to stern. The lighthouse had linked them to land,
now they were cut off, abandoned. Ewan had not
been entirely surprised that Andrew had run away;
he had refused to go looking for him as May had
wanted, but losing their light source, this was a real
disaster. The *Sunny Buoy* was now lost in the

darkness. Ewan scrutinised Ballydog. Although all the houses and the fish finger factory were dark, the street lights of Ballydog still burned tungsten orange and the lights in the windows of the lighthouse still glowed. There had been no power cut.

'Maybe we should go back!' shouted May.

'We're not going back,' responded Ewan.

Less than a minute later the light came back on. Ewan breathed out in relief.

At the lighthouse, Weir climbed back up to the platform and trained the spotlight on the boat again.

Ewan forgot his relief as his knees buckled and he was pressed into the deck. The *Sunny Buoy* was being tugged up another swell. Ewan had the pit-of-the-stomach sensation that goes with sudden, sharp, upward movement. The boards were beyond creaking, they screeched from bow to stern. Rotten pieces of the deck crumbled. The hull was stretched to its limit as it rode the crest and slid down the other side.

'Good job the light's back on us!' yelled May as Ewan struggled back to his place at the mast. 'Thought we were in trouble there for a second!'

White bullets of water whipped off the bow and stung Ewan's face. Another swell hit. And another. He held grimly to the mast and watched the sea ahead for a sign of the creature. The force of gravity would press him into the deck, then try to lift him into the air, then press him down again.

It must be soon now, thought Ewan. *Soon, soon.*

*   *   *

178

The swells invading Ballydog Bay were greatly reduced by the time they hit town, but they were still tall enough to throw about Ballydog's fleet. Cables were snapping and whipping across the pier. The metal hulls of the boats were banging together and resounding like great bells. The water level had risen and threatened to flood the town square. Waves broke on the sea wall and washed as far as the Lobster's Cage.

The face of the creature was fifteen kilometres away.

A window of the hotel exploded and a torrent of greenery poured out. The Dimwheat shot vines in all directions. One wrapped around a telegraph pole, others spread upward and dragged slates off the roof. As they spread, the vines sprouted new leaves at incredible speed. Inside, the door of room seven popped out of its frame and greenery burst into the hallway.

'Frank! That sounds serious,' pleaded Mrs Boyle. 'Get up and investigate.'

Mr Boyle had the blankets pulled up over his head. He had already ignored the crashing coming from the fleet, and bizarre noises coming from his own hotel would still not persuade him to get out of bed.

'I didn't hear a thing,' responded Mr Boyle, 'besides, I'm ill. That stew! I'll never eat anything like that again.'

Mrs Boyle could not bring herself to move either. She burrowed under the blankets and held her pillow over her ears.

Throughout Ballydog, people were doing the same thing.

CHAPTER TWENTY-NINE

'We've no time for proper flying lessons, Hunter,' said Andrew, 'we're going to smash that light right now.'

The Hunter stood. Andrew stood in front of him, facing the same direction, and stepped backwards onto the steel toecaps of the Hunter's boots.

'Hang on to me and I'll take charge of this,' said Andrew. The jetpack was still on the Hunter's back but he could not handle it because of his broken arm. Instead, the Hunter wrapped his good arm around Andrew and Andrew took the guide stick in his right hand. He would control their flight. Luckily not much control would be required. They were only going to go straight. Straight up.

The Hunter was far from happy with the plan but went along with it as he did not have a better one. He clamped Andrew tight against him and looked up the sheer side of the lighthouse.

'Okay, boy, press the ignition button when you are readieeeeeee . . .'

The plasma ignited and they soared up the tower, leaving a burning pink scratch in the air. To stop them tearing into the wall Andrew threw his feet out and he had the sensation of running up the lighthouse. They bounded up the tower and were at the top in ten strides. Then they were over the top and still going.

'CUT IT!' the Hunter screamed in Andrew's ear.

Andrew took his finger off the propulsion

button. The engine coughed and the heat behind their legs shrank and vanished. They dropped out of the sky like stones. They landed directly on top of the light's casing and tumbled down inside the guard rail. The Hunter's fall was broken by the jetpack and Andrew's fall was broken by the Hunter. They lay dazed in a pile for a moment. Then the Hunter shoved Andrew off him, slipped out of the straps of the jetpack, leaving it lying on the platform, and stood up against the guard rail.

'Now, where is the off-switch for this thing?' he asked.

The beam of light burned bright all around them. This close to the source of the intense beam it felt as if it was illuminating the insides of their heads. Its intensity meant Andrew and the Hunter did not see Weir coming at them from the other side of the light.

Andrew looked out to the *Sunny Buoy*. He saw how helpless it was. The sea beyond was starting to swell again. More than a wave, it was as if the ocean wanted to be a mountain.

Using his good arm, the Hunter aimed his pistol directly into the mouth of the Beamer. He was squeezing the trigger when Weir's hands, body and then contorted, hateful face burst into the scope of the light. He seized the Hunter's arm and threw him sideways. The pistol fired with a crack and a burning smell but the bullet missed the light, took a chip out of the guard rail and ricocheted off into the night. The pistol, broken from the Hunter's grip, sailed out after the bullet. Andrew dived for the weapon but it fell beyond his fingertips. Weir and the Hunter struggled, locked together, bouncing between the light and the guard rail.

181

Weir grabbed the Hunter's broken arm and twisted it in an unnatural direction. The Hunter was paralysed by agony. Weir took the opportunity to kick the Hunter's feet from under him and throw him over the side. Andrew saw the expression on the Hunter's face for a split second, it seemed to say, 'Oh no, not again.' Then he fell.

But he was not gone, not yet. The Hunter was hanging onto the edge of the platform by one arm, his other arm dangling uselessly by his side. Weir saw he was not quite rid of his enemy. He stamped repeatedly on his fingers. The whole platform rattled. Weir looked like an overgrown, and psychotically spoilt, child.

'I told you to get off my property,' he said.

Andrew tackled Weir. 'You're crazy,' he yelled, 'it's not your lighthouse and it's not your bay.'

Weir shoved him off easily. Andrew landed face down on the jetpack.

'I was taking care of the bay before you were even born,' Weir said. 'And I'll be taking care of it after you're gone. What are a few lives to save a town and its whole future?' He grabbed the boy by the collar and tried to pull him up.

'They *are* the future!' shouted Andrew. He wrapped one arm around the heavy jetpack to stop Weir lifting him. The jetpack was his anchor. He knew what Weir intended to do once he had him. He was going to throw him over the side. Weir dragged the boy along the platform, trying to shake him from the jetpack. For good measure he stepped again on the Hunter's fingers as he went by. The Hunter was frantically kicking into the plasterwork beneath the platform, attempting to make some kind of toehold. With his one free

182

hand Andrew tore at the pockets on the sides of the jetpack. He needed a weapon, something heavy, anything. As he pulled, all sorts of things fell out: bullets, cables, maps, but nothing that could save him.

Determined to separate Andrew from the jetpack, Weir seized him by both shoulders and prepared to wrench him up with his full strength.

'You don't need that thing to fly,' he said in Andrew's ear.

Andrew's fingers found the smallest pocket and fumbled with its contents. He barely knew what he had found. All his actions were automatic. Andrew let go of the jetpack so that when Weir, using all his might, pulled him he came away unexpectedly easily and they both staggered backwards.

'GOT YOU!' Weir screamed.

Andrew spun around and pushed the palm of his hand against Weir's mouth, as if all he wanted was to make Weir shut it. This amused Weir. He laughed in Andrew's face.

Then he burped.

It was a loud burp and took Weir completely by surprise. He let go of Andrew and placed one hand on his stomach and the other on his chest. Loud rumbling emerged from his body. His stomach could actually be seen to churn. The look on Weir's face was confusion, rapidly pitching into panic.

'What have you done to me?' he demanded of Andrew.

Andrew was himself disturbed at what he had done. He backed away from Weir, shaking his head.

'I'm sorry,' he said.

He opened his hand. Half a dozen small seeds lay in his palm. He had knocked two, maybe three of the Dimwheat seeds into Weir's mouth.

'I think it will be quick now, Mr Weir,' said Andrew quietly.

The Dimwheat, germinated by the moisture of Weir's stomach, reacted immediately to the approach of the vast sea creature. Weir opened his mouth to speak but was unable to form words. Only sickening strangled noises emerged, followed by a thin green shoot. Horrified, Weir watched a plant grow from his mouth. He staggered back along the platform, in and out of the light beam, but there was nowhere to hide from this. His stomach expanded in violent jolts. There was the sound of ripping, it might have been his clothes, it might not. He fell against the guard rail. Green shoots pushed through his pullover, green sheened with red. Weir stepped up onto the guard rail's first rung. Tall, and top heavy with the plant, as soon as Weir leaned forward he was gone over the side.

It would take about three seconds for a man, falling from the top of Ballydog's lighthouse, to hit the ground. Weir was dead before he hit the ground.

CHAPTER THIRTY

Ewan and May knew fear now. The Atlantic horizon rolled towards them and, worse, it was way above their heads, a cliff of water. Ewan hugged the mast. The ten-metre swell dragged the boat up and up until the knife-edge seconds when it hovered on the crest. The propeller made a different sound when, for a few seconds, it was turning in air and not in water. Then they slid down the other side, the bow disappearing in black water before pulling up, sending seawater crashing across the deck. The loose water almost dislodged Ewan before washing through the door of the wheelhouse. Ewan, on his knees hugging the mast, and May, clinging to the wheel, watched the next swell approach. It was twice as tall as the last.

Just then May felt a small but furious pounding begin between her ears. It did not form words, only a beat.

'Fire the flares!' screamed May from the wheelhouse. 'I CAN FEEL IT! IT'S ON US!'

Ewan could not see anything, but he took May's word for it. He let go of the mast to gather all the cords.

Ferociously, the *Sunny Buoy* was thrown up by the next swell. There was a nauseating splitting noise, like an old tree being felled. Somewhere below deck the *Sunny Buoy* was rending apart. The deck was sucked from under Ewan's feet as it went to forty-five degrees. He flew through the door of the wheelhouse and ended in a heap behind May. She was hanging onto the wheel, her feet clear off the floor. She looked down at Ewan.

'Did you?'

He showed her what was in his hands. The flares' ripcords had come clean away in his fists. They had all been pulled. The flares were pumping one tall plume into the air. Already the beam from the lighthouse was converting the smoke signal into a glowing orange cloud.

'There's no way it'll miss that,' said May, as her feet touched the floor again.

The *Sunny Buoy* broached the top of the swell. Planks snapped. The propeller made a dry note. From the open sea they could see the next swell approaching, it was a kilometre away. It was almost the height of the lighthouse.

'Come on then,' said May, 'show yourself.'

The Big Hungry, the Ancient Traveller, the Leveller, there were many names for the creature that burst from that swell. The one-hundred-tonne wall of water ripped apart and turned to rain. May and Ewan's eyes widened. It was like the end of the world. The creature's black-hole mouth fell open and a hive of heaving tongues, each a hundred metres long, tasted the air. To the right and left of the mouth were its eyes. Grey, lifeless pits that saw but did not understand.

Then it was gone.

The lighthouse beam was cut again.

Everything went black. The sea creature could not see them. They could not see it. The smoke cloud above the *Sunny Buoy* blended with the night sky. It was invisible.

The swell the *Sunny Buoy* was riding poured back the way it had come, rushing to fill the space the creature created by raising its face out of the sea.

The sea creature had not even seen the *Sunny Buoy* before the light was cut for the second time. Its brain operated very slowly and it had not registered the sacrifice it had been offered. The *Sunny Buoy* and its signal had been snatched away too quickly.

The youngsters' plan had failed. This was no

186

surprise as it was based on a lie, but Weir's plan, his true plan, had failed as well.

The sea creature's mouth opened wider. It still intended taking Ballydog. It did not even see the tiny craft before it. Through eyes that have never blinked, it looked towards its real target. The mouth of Ballydog Bay was punched wider as it entered. Under the water, huge boulders were ground into pebbles. Instinct told the creature where to go. Instinct told it what to do once it got there. Leave nothing standing.

May and Ewan fell to the floor of the wheelhouse and clung to each other.

'Why!' cried May. 'Why would Weir leave us in the dark?'

'I don't know,' said Ewan, but already he suspected that events had followed a plan, just not their plan. 'Weir,' said Ewan, in a voice so low it was almost a thought. Suddenly he knew that, one way or another, they had been used. He had been so eager to take his stand, so happy to be *chosen*, that Weir had been able to fool him.

A dead wind from the bottom of the sea blew over them. It came from the creature's mouth. The seawater collapsed from under the *Sunny Buoy* and the boat was left gliding through the open air, turning a slow revolution as it travelled. Ewan and May gripped each other tight. A gust of stale air whistled through the door.

'It's going to swallow us,' whispered Ewan.

The *Sunny Buoy*'s last port of call was the monster's mouth. Two faint screams emerged from the vortex of its throat.

The tips of rough tongues slapped at the hull of the *Sunny Buoy* as it flew over. The vessel hit their riving roots and was bounced from one tongue to another, all the while sliding down the creature's throat. The mast snapped away like a matchstick. The generator and washroom separated and bounced over the side. The boat ploughed through the thick coating of the creature's gullet. Washes of slime shot right and left from the driven bow. The *Sunny Buoy* slowed a little in the mire but its momentum still drove it deeper. In the wheelhouse, May and Ewan hung on to each other as the *Sunny Buoy* disintegrated around them. Down, down, down they slid. There was nowhere darker than where they were going. It was the darkest place on earth.

CHAPTER THIRTY-ONE

For two seconds Andrew was frozen by indecision. Should he smash the light immediately or help the Hunter first? They were both pressing concerns. The flares on the *Sunny Buoy* had just been set off. It was as Weir had calculated. The smoke plume glowed huge, easily visible from the lighthouse and equally visible from the open sea. An enormous swell was pouring towards the *Sunny Buoy* from the ocean. But the Hunter was hanging by one set of blackened fingers and could not for much longer. Then it hit Andrew. He did not have to smash the light. He only had to point the Beamer away from the boat. A sharp kick and the Beamer was aimed harmlessly up into the sky. The *Sunny Buoy* was hidden in the darkness again.

'Heave,' breathed the Hunter. It took three

attempts for Andrew to pull him up. Luckily the Hunter was not a big man.

Lying on the platform, panting, the Hunter looked seaward. Nothing could be seen out there.

'I would not say your friends are exactly *safe*,' he said, 'but they are better in the dark than lit up like Christmas. The monster is close.'

The Dimwheat plants, spouting from the around the base of the lighthouse, were already huge. They wrapped themselves around the tower, winding higher by the minute. Plate-sized leaves flapped in the wind.

'So now,' said the Hunter. 'Time to worry about us, ya? There is no sacrifice so your town will be destroyed. Sorry. But we make good flying team me and you, let us fly inland, ya? . . . Boy?'

Andrew was already strapping himself into the jetpack.

'No, I'm going to go get my friends,' he said. 'I'll come back here for you after I've got them safe.'

The Hunter groaned and let his head fall back on the platform, but he did not protest more than that. The jetpack probably had enough thrust to lift three small people, it had carried Andrew and himself without difficulty. But he knew there was a good chance the monster would pick on the lighthouse to destroy first. Research indicated that monsters were attracted to large buildings. Andrew would not have enough time to airlift the others and be back in time for him.

This may be the end of a glorious career, thought the Hunter.

'Ya,' he said. 'Go get them. I will stay here and watch what this monster does. Call it research.'

Andrew was not able to stand in the jetpack. He

189

started it while in a crouched position. He launched like a firework. Out of control, he made a wide loop in the air. The G-forces on his body were incredible but his adrenalin kept him conscious. He stabilised, attempted to turn seaward but instead veered up over the hills, in completely the wrong direction. He banked left, and almost crashed into the telegraph poles along the roadside before managing to pull up. Passing over the centre of Ballydog, he saw the town square was flooding. Cars parked on the square were being shifted about by surges. Nobody was doing anything to stop the flood damage. Not a single person could be seen. Andrew looked in the direction of the estate and his own home; it was dark and helpless. He thought of his family in their rooms.

Andrew lost control of the jetpack again. He lost height.

'UP, UP, UP!' he roared at himself.

It was not easy to be delicate with the guide stick while the town square raced towards him. For a split second he imagined life as a pancake. Throwing his whole body into it, he shot sideways, the toes of his shoes striking off the surface of the new pier.

'UP!'

He shot between the masts of the fleet. They were swaying wildly. Then all he could see was black water. Then he was lost.

Andrew was underwater.

But with a watery explosion he was back in the open air. He had not crashed down into the bay but had collided with a high wave and shot straight out the back of it. Andrew's relief burst out in a shout. He pulled up and skimmed the crest of the next wave. His eyes streamed as cold air and salt water dashed his face, but he was back in control. Andrew aimed for the mouth of the bay and increased his speed.

Andrew did not know it, but he was almost like Perseus. Perseus had sandals with wings to make him fly. Andrew had the jetpack. Perseus had the Medusa's head to fight the sea creature with. Unfortunately Andrew had nothing like that.

CHAPTER THIRTY-TWO

'Ye alive?' whispered May.

'I'm not sure,' replied Ewan.

The *Sunny Buoy* had come to a halt. It was on the flat now, the part of the creature's length that was still on the floor of the bay. Ewan and May were in the wheelhouse, bruised but breathing. It was pure black down there, but they could feel themselves and each other. Were they really still alive? Or was this the place dead souls went?

'What about you?' Ewan asked. 'Are you alive?'

'I think so,' said May. 'I'm hurting all over so I must be. Where are we?'

'We're inside it, May, we're in its belly.'

It was cold and damp in there, it was a cold-blooded creature. The darkness was absolute. Eyes would never adjust to it. Although they could not see to confirm it their other senses told them they were in a vast chamber. The *Sunny Buoy* had no power for its lights. The generator and engine were smashed and scattered. Their world was

191

pitch-black now. The air was a rotten stench, thick with bacteria and viruses. It hugged them slickly. There was no breeze, no relief.

'This is bad,' said May.

They began to slowly pull themselves out of the crumpled heap they had landed in.

'Rats,' said May.

'Where?' said Ewan, his voice pitched high in fright.

'I don't know, close but not on the boat. They seem big. Bigger than normal rats.'

Ewan realised that it was through her mind she felt them.

'What . . . what are they thinking?'

MeatMeatMeatMeatMeatMeatMeatMeatMeatMeat.

'I think they're hungry,' said May.

Ewan scrambled for where the torch was kept hanging, behind the wheel. The walls of the wheelhouse were semi-collapsed and the door completely ripped off, but the torch was still snugly fitted in its place. His fingers found it.

'Was that the rats?' said Ewan. They had both heard it. A loud wet squishing sound.

'No, the rats are running away, it's something else . . .' May concentrated harder.

There were more squelching noises, like the sounds a boot makes as it sinks into a swamp and is then pulled back out. Footsteps?

'What's that?' breathed May, trying to keep her voice low. Not easy to do with the fear.

'It's the torch, I have it in my hands, it probably still works—'

'*No*,' breathed May. 'We have to stay hidden. And . . . I don't want to know what they look like.'

'They?'

192

'They're animals but they think like people,' said May, 'or they're people and they think like animals.'

There was a slight shift in the *Sunny Buoy*'s position and the sound of somebody heaving themselves out of a mud bath. Out over the bow and stern they heard other squelching movements. And what was that, a watery cough? The boat dipped again. They were being boarded. Ewan and May sank against the back of the wheelhouse, all four of their hands on the torch, still switched off, as if it was a holy talisman. They pointed it towards the door, but even with four hands they could not stop it shaking.

From out on deck came loud sniffing noises.

'Ewan, they are thinking about us. They're giving us names. But they're not goin' to be nice to us.'

Judging by the loudness of the sniffs they, whatever they were, must have had huge nostrils. Ewan realised that he and May were being located by their scent.

May felt Ewan's thumb move onto the torch's button.

'No,' she said, her voice low and urgent, 'they're not goin' to be nice to us.'

But Ewan was the kind of boy who always had to *know*. He pressed the button and the torch shone out.

This was the creature's stomach.

The *Sunny Buoy* had landed at the base of a hill. A heap of overturned boats, chunks of buildings and the bones of whales. The whole thing was sunk at the bottom of a massive chamber, like a living cathedral, its walls heaving in and out. A shanty

193

town had grown in this heap. Through this town of the damned, paths wound between crude shelters and heaving mounds of black goo. There were feeding places, large nests made of stomach lining and naked humanoid figures groping around. The whole mess crawled with life, if that existence could be called life. Dark shapes scuttled out of the light beam. Mutated creatures howled at its brightness. Rats the size of dogs stared back into the torchlight; it glinted off their beady eyes.

The people, if they were people, on the deck of the *Sunny Buoy* were not alarmed by the torchlight. They did not turn away or cover their eyes. This was strange because their eyes were huge, like two white eggs in their heads. They stared straight at May and Ewan but did not seem to see them. It was their wide nostrils they were following. They moved across the deck, leaving damp trails behind them. There were fourteen of them.

Ewan and May were beyond shaking with fear. Their bodies froze. The blood stopped flowing in their veins. They were shutting down. They were better off going to sleep, maybe they would be lucky and never wake up again.

As well as large eyes and nostrils the humanoids had fat mouths, thick lips and no teeth, like frogs. Most of them were hairless. Some walked upright, others moved on all fours. When they brushed against each other they began to shove and fight.

The humanoids were the descendants of the people swallowed by the creature over the centuries. For generations this lost branch of the human race had de-evolved in this pit of badness. This was their universe. They no longer had language. They had no idea there was an outside world where their forbears had once come from. They did not know of the sun. Living in constant darkness made their eyes large but by now most of them were blind. What use did evolution have for eyes in this place? All these humanoids did with their lives was crawl about, bump into one another and try to find something to eat.

Today was different from the usual cold grind of their existences. May and Ewan smelled fresh and warm. Completely different to anything they had come across before. Once in a lucky generation's life the sea creature would awaken, feed and then there would be fresh things for the humanoids to pounce on. Like food and building materials, maybe even a boost to the population.

The humanoids sniffed the air and stepped into the wheelhouse. Those at the back pulled and kicked at the competition. One of them, a crawler, moved fast between the legs of those nearest the front. It smacked its lips, tasting the air only centimetres away from Ewan's face. Ewan pressed back into himself, his face a mask of stifled disgust. Then the humanoid swung its face towards May. It extended its wet fingers and stroked her shoulder, then wrapped its hand around her wrist. She was transfixed by pure cold terror. The humanoid licked its lips and pulled up its slack lower jaw. Its thick lips moved up into its cheeks. It was happy. It was smiling.

Plop.

Then it tugged May closer to its face and, with a large grey tongue, it licked her arm.

Plop, plop.

Outside it was raining bricks. They plopped into

195

the mud around the *Sunny Buoy*. One. Two, three. Then suddenly dozens. One bounced high off the deck and caused excitement among the humanoids out there. But the humanoid holding May could not be distracted by anything. It kept smiling.

These were the happiest moments of its life. They were also its last.

The chimney of Ballydog's fish finger factory fell out of the darkness. It had been swallowed whole. Vertically, it went straight through the deck of the *Sunny Buoy*, hammering humanoids into floor. The front of the wheelhouse was torn away and May was released as the humanoid was knocked straight through the deck. For a few seconds May and Ewan were presented with the upside-down chimney, teetering where the front of the wheelhouse had been. Then the *Sunny Buoy* went to pieces. The stern rolled backwards, catapulting Ewan and May over the side. The torch was flung away and all was black again. They hit the cold mire with a squelch and it immediately sucked them in. The sides of the chimney unpeeled and bricks rained down.

The sea creature was feasting. The fish finger factory, the largest building in town, was where it began. A huge chunk of the roof sailed down and carved a deep channel in the swamp as it landed. Any of them could have been killed any second, but six or seven of the humanoids longed so much to touch the visitors they ignored the danger. They waded through the slime and dug in it for the youngsters' arms and legs, each fighting to claim one for itself. May and Ewan were snapped back out of the slime and stretched in all directions. They called each other's names, but were powerless to help themselves or each other. All around bricks and smashed machinery were splashing down, a rain of destruction. The humanoids did not care. These sweet-smelling prizes were worth the risk. The sudden arrival of these warm bodies was the most exciting thing that had ever happened to them. Smelling the newcomers, feeling their warm dry flesh, was the nearest thing to joy they had ever experienced. They pulled harder.

'MAY!'

'EWWWWAN!'

There was a flash in the sky like a star being born. The star spiralled, shook and descended towards them.

Could it be?

It was Andrew, flying in the jetpack. Still an awkward flier but improving fast. A final staggering swoop and he was three metres above them. Andrew banked hard and spun a circle. The heat from the jetpack terrified the humanoids and sent them flying. May and Ewan were dropped back into the swamp.

'Reach up, grab the straps and hang on tight!' Andrew shouted. Desperately they grabbed at the jetpack.

'Lower, lower,' screamed May. She was up to her waist in the mud. Ewan, hanging on a strap with one arm, grabbed her and raised her a few vital centimetres. She threw her arms through the other strap. With a loud wet slurp Andrew tugged his friends from the swamp. May's wellingtons were left behind.

'Hold on tight,' yelled Andrew, 'we're going to go fast!'

They zoomed upwards. Andrew swerved right and left to avoid chunks of the factory falling towards them. They flew as near to the top of the throat as possible. In a whirl of concrete and machinery half the ground floor of the factory thundered beneath them. Then the taxidermist's van shot past, quickly followed by cars, and for the briefest of seconds the youngsters felt they were flying above a motorway. The freezer units, neatly shorn in two, bounced back and forth against the walls of the throat, stomach-bound. The Old Man of the Sea was flung past, released from his glass case.

Not the best grave for him, thought May, *but better than on display.*

Then there was nothing. The flood of demolition stopped. The youngsters were no longer flying upwards but horizontally then downwards, following the wide tunnel of the creature's throat as it bent over Ballydog. They dived but as the creature's gullet whooshed open the onslaught of smashed architecture began again. They dropped through a chaos of concrete chunks, ripped pipes and walling. Everything spun in a motion of gulps. Around them the tongues of the creature snapped and writhed. Beneath their feet the factory's foundation was in pieces and spinning in a whirlpool of destruction.

Ewan and May closed their eyes, but Andrew kept his open.

Through an exploding wall they dived, through a shredded floor, through a hurricane of soil and sand.

They were out.

Andrew was leaning back into the jetpack as if

that would slow their descent. He cut the engine and they dropped two metres to freshly exposed bedrock. Clean air entered their lungs, then seawater. They were at the bottom of a hole where the factory used to be. The sea creature, enormous above them, blocked out the sky. The apocalyptic roar was deafening. Its legs, suspended uselessly in the air, rippled and clattered together. It raised its mouth to swallow again. Great falls of seawater crashed from its body and washed out its mouth. The hole was flooding, rapidly.

'Let's get out of here,' said May, spitting out water.

They clambered up the side of the hole but the water rose just as fast. Andrew dragged the jetpack behind him. At the top they fled, thinking only to get out from under the creature. Above them its tongues snapped and grabbed at things, each tongue in itself a monster. The youngsters ran in the direction of the old pier and the lighthouse. It seemed like the safest direction. The sea creature swung its face through the sky, back and forth as if to say, *what next*? It was in no hurry. It had all night.

'There's nobody in sight,' shouted Andrew. 'Did they all run away?'

'I think they're hiding!' called Ewan.

'Ye wanna go to your family?' May yelled to Andrew. They all looked at the jetpack dragging behind Andrew. Water sloshed from its combustion chamber.

'I'll have to run,' he said.

'Me too,' said Ewan. He looked towards the estate and thought of his mother alone there.

May stood like a girl torn in two directions,

which was exactly what she was. She looked in the direction of the Batter and her grandmother's cottage, then over at the Lobster's Cage. Her dad would be in there. The bar, the Batter, the bar.

In the end she did not have to make that decision. Events took over.

There was a muffled boom and a patch of water along the sea creature's side foamed high.

'Something's happening,' shouted Ewan, 'look!'

The foam ran white, then green and black.

The creature's body had been punctured, but due to the smallness of its brain it was a full fifteen seconds before it registered an itch from its side. As if in slow motion the creature swung its face around, shooting a torrential rainstorm into Ballydog. Bile was leaking from the tear. The creature's legs clanged against one another in what might have been frustration.

BOOM.

Another underwater explosion. Water fizzled white and then turned the colour of the sea creature's guts. Fifteen seconds later the creature shuddered and this shudder passed along its length like a slow, but immensely powerful, whiplash. Its body struck something under the water. A hard object.

The bow of the USS *Deep Trouble* was thrown above the surface and its stern crashed into the floor of the bay. Some of the crew hit the roof before rolling down the gangways. Captain Reef hung on to a console until the craft stopped rocking.

'Damage report,' he barked.

He pulled his cap down tighter.

Day and night the submarine had followed the

creature. After they had discovered it, Captain Reef was given orders to follow and investigate the new life form. Captain Reef never liked the mission. He thought longingly of his torpedoes while trailing the creature all the way from the southern Atlantic. That night he took a risk by overtaking it and cruising into Ballydog Bay. His navigators had calculated that this was its most likely destination. It was just as well, since some of the creature's length was still out under the ocean and its width was blocking the mouth of the bay. They could not have come in after it. Reef was relieved to have finally gone to war with the creature. It had attacked an innocent town in a friendly nation and he had no option. At least that would be his excuse. At last his beautiful, sleek, deadly submarine was fulfilling its potential. Millions of dollars of brutal hardware and tinkling, cunning software was doing what it did best. Finally, this was what the machine was meant for. This was what Reef was meant for. This was war. Due to the tight confines of the bay the *Deep Trouble* had fired torpedoes at a much closer range than was advisable. The creature had struck back surprisingly fast.

'Bulkhead damage, sir,' the officer reported. 'The propulsor is crushed. Possible fires. Recommend immediate surfacing.'

Reef watched loose objects sliding along the tilted floor.

'We're half-surfaced already. Bring us up. Get another couple of MK 50s in the tubes. We can still keep shooting. We may have too.'

All one-hundred-and-ten metres of the *Deep Trouble* broke the surface. Its bow splashed downward, sending waves in all directions. Although it was a small object the sea creature knew it required attention.

'Captain Reef, sir, we have to override all procedure to fire at this range.'

'So what's new?'

A torpedo launched. It skimmed the water before going under and piercing the creature, but the explosion did as much shockwave damage to the submarine as it did to the monster. The *Deep Trouble* shook in an internal explosion. The rear hatches blew off and smoke pumped into the air. Reef ordered more torpedoes, he knew nothing else to do.

'Fire again, again!' screamed Reef.

Did Reef really think he could kill this giant? Maybe it was just his duty to try. The sea creature would win the fight without even knowing it was fighting. The *Deep Trouble* had no chance. Short of nuclear weapons, the sea creature could take any wound it could inflict. It will have a hundred years to heal, and heal it will. The creature rose above the submarine, the chamber of its mouth forming a swirling gale.

'Sir,' reported an officer, 'we are lit up!'

It was true. The external monitors showed they were in a pool of light, probably created by a spotlight.

'Who? From where?' asked Reef.

May, Andrew and Ewan knew the answers to those questions. They were watching the battle from the track to the old pier. They had the shock of seeing the submarine break the surface and sustain more damage. Then they saw a beam of light move over the submarine and stay there.

'Hunter is aiming the light at them,' said Andrew. 'I left him on the top.'

The spotlight lit up the smoke clouds pouring from the submarine's stern. The cloud glowed and got bigger each second. The sea creature looked blankly at what it found, then was overcome by an ancient instinct.

Sacrifice.

At last it was being offered a sacrifice.

A great vacuum whipped up waves as the sea creature stretched its mouth wide. Then it fell upon the submarine and dragged it down into its maw.

CHAPTER THIRTY-THREE

In Washington DC stood a memorial to the crew of USS *Deep Trouble*. The names of the crew were carved into marble, along with the words: 'Missing in Action'. With that wall of marble, bugle calls and salutes the ultimate sacrifice of the crew was honoured, but few people knew how real a sacrifice it was. They really had been sacrificed, to the ancient sea creature. The submarine was sizable and not as easy to break up as a building. The creature dragged it out of Ballydog Bay, flattened it and gulped several times to get it down.

Satisfied, the creature sank back under the ocean. It went to find a place to rest until the next time it was called. It may have marched for a week to find a suitable site. When it settled it became the basis of a local ecology. Banks of anemones and seagrasses grew across its mineral-rich back. Shoals of fish nibbled at its wounds. Coral crept over it. Eventually it would be a long ridge in the seabed again. Deep asleep, the Ancient Traveller was returned to the sea, and to its myth.

Having been completely washed down, Ballydog gleamed in the light of next morning. The sky was cloudless, it too seemed to have been scrubbed clean. Down by the sea the people found the remains of a calamity. There had been flooding during the night; the water had receded but by then cars had vanished and wide cracks zigzagged through the town square. Trawlers were dented and their portholes cracked. Two had gone completely, probably sunk. One trawler had been thrown clear out of the bay and lay at an angle where the cars should have been. Its rounded hull meant that, despite its size, little children were able to push it and make it rock gently, like a giant cradle.

Most shocking of all was a yawning crater where the fish finger factory had stood. This was an astounding absence. The factory had been big, and so important to the people of the town that it had always seemed even bigger. Now it had vanished. From now on the view from many of Ballydog's windows would be different. In one night the skyline had changed. The factory and its tall chimney had been taken away and Ballydog's centre of gravity had shifted.

The people of Ballydog left their houses and walked to the square. They came in a procession, quiet and humbled, down the road from the estate. They stood around the gaping hole where the factory had been.

204

' "Deserves to be ripped out of the ground," that's what she said, wasn't it?' said McKann.

'Indeed, those were her very words.'

'The soft-headed one was right?' said Mrs Hooard.

'No, not soft-headed, wise I'd say she is,' suggested Cody Savage.

'A visionary even, I'd say a visionary, wouldn't you, Fitz? Sorry, Mr Fitzpatrick?'

'She was right anyway,' Fitz said, 'that's the main thing.'

Fitz stood among everyone else. Nobody wanted a speech this morning. There was a curious expression on Fitz's face, a similar expression shared by all. Not an unhappy expression, nor a happy one. It was something like the expression of a just-born baby, blank and wide open. Everything was new.

All morning the people moved around the town square. Talking, thinking, examining. There was an atmosphere of shock, they were a bunch of confused survivors. Everybody thought they had an idea of what had happened but nobody *really* knew, and nobody asked. Some of the children squealed about seeing a sea monster from their bedroom windows, taking the factory in its mouth. Their parents hushed them, but thought their children might be right all the same. Why not? Anything was possible now.

Along the shore the lighthouse was wrapped in thick vines, its whitewash hardly to be seen, but the growth was already turning brown and losing its grip on the tower. The front of the hotel was also coated in a giant dying weed.

Ewan's mother was looking up at its brown

curling leaves when Ewan stepped up beside her. He touched her arm.

'I think it is an improvement,' Ewan's mother said to him. 'It was such an ugly-looking kip before.'

'Do you mean just the hotel or the whole town?' asked Ewan.

His mother laughed. 'Both, I suppose. It's a lucky thing. We'll be here for a few more months yet you know.'

'That's all right. I don't think it is *so* bad here now.'

'I'm glad.'

'Do you mind if I go look for my friends?' asked Ewan.

'Friends?' asked his mother. 'Sure, go on ahead.'

Andrew had to be in town somewhere. Ewan saw his parents. They were leading the twins to look at the pit where the factory had been. The little boys were curiously unimpressed by it. Ewan also saw May's dad, sitting alone on the front step of the Lobster's Cage.

Heiferon was standing at one side of the square, pale and subdued.

'Mr Heiferon, have you seen Andrew? I'm looking for him.'

'Andrew? No, I have not,' said Heiferon. 'And no school today, bucko. Not with all these . . .' he gestured at the townsfolk looking into pit while he sought a way to describe the scene, 'all these changes going on.'

'School tomorrow though?' asked Ewan. Suddenly he longed for normality. Even Ballydog normality would do.

'What do you care? Haven't seen you in a

206

couple of days anyway, have I?'

'I had something important to do,' said Ewan, then he thought for a moment. 'Well, maybe it was more like something important happened to me and I just happened to be there at the time.'

'That's fine,' said Heiferon and he looked seaward. 'Yes, there will be school tomorrow,' he said, 'being as I happen to be here too.'

Then Heiferon pointed with his thumb and said, 'There's the brat over there . . .'

Andrew was standing on the end of the pier, gazing into the waters of Ballydog Bay. He had at his feet a strange contraption. Like a large backpack, but of dented steel. Ordinarily it would have drawn the attention of townsfolk, but today it went unnoticed. Andrew looked down at his hands, still stained from the night before. He flexed them as if seeing them for the first time.

'Life-taker,' he said quietly.

'Lifesaver,' said Ewan as he stepped up beside him.

Andrew looked at Ewan, then back at his hands. Andrew was remembering how he had ended the life of the lighthouse keeper.

'It's not so terrible. You're a hero, I'd say,' said Ewan.

Andrew just shrugged. 'Never again though,' he said.

'What are you doing with this?'

'I was going to try and fix it,' he said, 'but don't think I want the thing any more.'

Andrew gave the jetpack a sharp kick.

'Will Mr Hunter be looking for it?' asked Ewan.

'Nah,' said Andrew. 'I met him this morning already, his arm was patched up and someone was driving him away. He was going to "slip back into the shadows", as he put it. He's long gone. He can probably buy a new jetpack with the money he makes, and his "connections". Me, I want a peaceful life.'

With his foot Andrew shunted the jetpack towards the edge of the pier.

'Sure?' asked Ewan.

'Sure,' said Andrew. The jetpack went over the edge and, with a long second of silent descent and a splash, it was gone.

*   *   *

The Batter was plastered in the leaves sucked from the trees during the night. May made her way up, carefully, she was still in her bare feet. When she reached the cottage of the Woman on the Hill she found the door open. She tapped on it lightly and looked in. The old woman was in her chair in the shadowy front room.

'Would ye like to come in, me dear?' she asked.

'Maybe ye'd like to come out?' said May.

The old woman laughed her dry laugh and pulled herself out of her chair. She was slightly stooped but used no walking stick. Her eyes squinted in the morning light.

'Just down to the garden gate will do me,' she said, 'we can sit on the wall and look about us.'

'Ye don't need to be frightened when I'm with ye,' said May earnestly.

The old woman laughed. 'I'm not frightened. Just old. I couldn't be bothered going further. The view is grand from here.'

She sat on the wall and lit a cigarette, offering

one to May.

'Do ye smoke?'

'No.'

'Look,' the old woman nodded towards magpies in the trees. 'They've come back already. Saw a badger this morning too.'

'I know why all the birds and animals went away,' said May. 'I'd like to tell ye about it.'

The Woman on the Hill had a glint in her eye. 'I think I know something of it already,' she said, 'but I'd like to hear the details anyways.'

'I know another thing I'd like to tell ye about too,' May went on, 'something even more important.'

The old woman's eyes now shone bright. 'I know about that already too,' she said. 'Today is the day of *coming back*. Some things, like the birds, were only gone a few days. I missed them, but it weren't so bad. Someone else has been gone for years and I have ached day and night with missing her.'

May tried to say something but choked a little instead. She jumped to her feet.

'It was me dad kept us apart,' she shouted, 'I hate him!'

'Ah now be careful there,' said her grandmother. 'Can ye forgive?'

'Don't know,' said May, but the white light behind her eyes subdued a little. 'He's useless though, ain't he? Weak?'

Her grandmother bowed her head. 'Ye can come live with me if ye'd like,' she said.

'I'd love that,' said May, 'for a wee while.'

'Are ye going somewhere?'

'Aye,' said May. She stood and looked up into the trees. 'Don't ask me where. But away from

Ballydog. I wanna find out what's out there, and
. . .' May tapped her own forehead, 'what's in here.
Ballydog won't help me with that, will it?'

'Things are going to get better in Ballydog,' said
her grandmother with a smile, 'that's what I
predict.'

'Aye . . . maybe.' With her big toe May poked at
the leaves pasted to the stones of the lane. 'I
wanna leave anyway. There're better places for
me.'

'All right then so,' said her grandmother, 'but
there's something very important ye'll need before
ye go find your fortune.'

'What?'

'Shoes and socks.'

May spent that night in the cottage, and the
night after that. Soon the cottage at the end of
the Batter was her home. Her dad went to live in
the estate. Sometimes May went to visit him. They
would drink tea at the kitchen table and, between
long silences, talk about what had gone wrong in
their lives, and what had gone right.

'I don't really blame him,' May explained to
Andrew and Ewan. 'I couldn't be bothered. He's
not a big thing in me life any more.'

This sounded a sad situation to the boys,
especially to Ewan, who was separated from his
father and longed to see him again. They
wondered how May could live by such different
rules.

Andrew and Ewan would visit May regularly in
her new home. Andrew understood May's wish to
leave but he thought he would always stay in
Ballydog. To him it was home, pure and simple. As
for Ewan, it did not matter if he wanted to leave or

210

not. Either way, the day was approaching when he would. His mother was due to give her testimony in his father's trial to help free him. 'We'll come visit you,' his friends told Ewan.

'I'd like to live in the city,' May said. 'It would be exciting.'

Andrew would shake his head at the thought. He had had enough excitement.

May's grandmother sat in her chair and laughed with enjoyment. It was great to hear talk of future possibilities going on in her own cottage. The freedom to dream and plan was vital. Listening to the three youngsters making plans the old woman knew it was truly better not knowing the future in advance. Not knowing the future was life itself. She saw the determination in May and knew she probably would leave Ballydog, and her, behind. But in the meantime May was busy about the place. Housekeeping, weeding the path, painting the walls and, most importantly, practising her talent. May would break up yesterday's bread and put it out by the garden gate for the forest birds. She would leave the front door open so she could watch them. May's grandmother did not complain, even if it was cold. It felt good to have the door open. It allowed in the breezes that blew from the sea.